EVERYTHING
FOR A DOG

ISBN 978-0-545-31393-3

12 11 10 9 8 7 6 5 4 3 2 1   10 11 12 13 14 15/0

Printed in the U.S.A.   40

First Scholastic printing, October 2010

Book design by Barbara Grzeslo

For my aunt,
Adele Vinsel

With special thanks to my nephew,
Henry McGrath

In memory of Kate McClelland

EVERYTHING
FOR A DOG

1. BONE

My tale begins with a tail. It is my earliest memory, this tail. I was twelve days old and my eyes had opened for the first time. I tried to focus them and I became aware of something moving, something black and white, something so intriguing that I bit it. It was a tail and it belonged to my sister, who yelped. I didn't have any teeth yet so I hadn't hurt her, but I had surprised her, my timid sister, Squirrel. Next I bit my mother, and she swatted me with her great brown paw. Then she drew me to her belly, and I curled into it, Squirrel pressed against my side.

Squirrel and I were the only surviving puppies in our litter. My mother, whose dog name was Stream, had given birth to three others, but only my sister and I had lived. Mother had waited until she saw that we were strong and then she had given us our names—Bone and Squirrel, two things of vital importance to her.

I am Bone.

Mother gave birth to Squirrel and me in a wheelbarrow in a shed on the property belonging to a family named

Merrion. We lived there in secret. Mother, who was a stray dog her entire short life, had roamed the countryside around Lindenfield for a long time searching for just the right spot in which to give birth to her puppies. She had started her search at the end of a winter that had been bitterly cold, but short. By the time the early spring arrived, bringing with it mild days and the scent of sunshine, the ice in the ponds was melting and the hibernating creatures were waking from their long sleeps, and Mother had selected the Merrions' land as the place on which to settle down for a while.

In truth, Mother selected well, but not perfectly. The Merrions, who visited their large house in the country only on the weekends, at least during the cooler weather, did not like animals—not wild animals, and not pets. Only Matthias, the middle Merrion child, wanted a pet, and he wanted one very badly. Mother and Squirrel and I and the stray cats that lived on the property took great care to remain out of sight of the Merrions. The other animals— the possums and squirrels and chipmunks, the deer and groundhogs and raccoons, the birds of all kinds, and the mother fox and her kits—did not attempt to hide, and occasionally they paid dearly for this.

But we had our shed and it was safe and cozy. The Merrions rarely went inside it. Also, two of the walls had been insulated at one time, so the shed was warm. And it was well ventilated since one window had been removed and the door remained permanently ajar. Mother had found a shelter that protected us from humans, rain, and predators, and was dry and warm but not too hot.

Mother wasn't the only creature who had discovered the shed. It was also populated by a number of stray cats and a great quantity of mice. The cats had taken up residence in the old nesting boxes for chickens that lined one wall. They crept through the holes into the little dark cubbies, still filled with straw, and gave birth to their kittens there. Mother kept clear of the nesting boxes, but the cats had to walk by her and the wheelbarrow and Squirrel and me on their way to and from the door. They tolerated us and we tolerated them.

For the first eleven days of my life I lived in darkness and silence, neither my eyes nor my ears open. My world was Mother's soft belly, her milk, and the wiggling presence of my sister. Squirrel and I squirmed and drank and dozed and jumped in our sleep. And then the next day dawned—the last dawn that I wouldn't be able to see for myself—and my eyes opened and there was that tail. I bit it and my sister yelped and for as long as we were together I was known as the brave one, the leader, and Squirrel was the timid one, the follower.

The day after my eyes opened, my ears opened too. Squirrel and I weren't very good at seeing and hearing at first. That took some time. But we grew bigger and fatter and stronger, and eventually the world of the shed became clear to us. I took notice of the cats and the mice and then of the bees and other flying insects. The mice and the insects were interesting. They could slip into places too small for Squirrel and me, and they could zip straight up walls and beams. I sat in our wheelbarrow and followed them with my eyes, wishing I could slip and zip and fly.

One day a pair of barn swallows dipped into the shed through the open window. With much chittering and cheeping and calling to each other, they then swooped in and out and in and out of that window for several days. Each time they returned to the shed they carried bits of straw or long pieces of grass in their beaks, and they began to fashion a muddy nest on the side of the beam directly above the wheelbarrow. Squirrel and I watched the nest building with interest. So did the cats. The nest had reached the height of half a small flowerpot, the roof beam forming its back wall, when one of the swallows zoomed through the window one afternoon and was caught in midair between the jaws of a yellow cat that had been waiting with great patience on an upper beam. The other swallow returned to the nest several more times before he realized his mate was missing. Then he stopped coming into the shed, and the nest remained unfinished.

Our shed was interesting, but as the weather grew

warmer I became curious about what was outside the walls. I especially wanted to know more about the mother fox, whose name, I think, was Mine. My mother spent a lot of time watching Mine, and I wondered why. She wasn't afraid of her, but I believe she felt threatened by her. Mother watched her especially closely when the Merrions were at home. When the Merrions were away, Mother paid less attention to her. I noticed that of all the animals that made their homes on the Merrions' property, Mine seemed least concerned with keeping herself hidden. I watched her walk haughtily through the yard at all hours of day and night, whether the Merrions were away or at home.

As the dramas of the swallows and Mine unfolded, and as a thousand smaller daily dramas occurred, Squirrel and I grew bigger and stronger, and one afternoon, Mother surprised us. Without any warning she nudged me over the edge of the wheelbarrow and I tumbled to the floor of the shed, landing on a pile of burlap sacks. Then she nudged Squirrel over the edge. Squirrel whimpered. She was afraid. But I was thrilled. Now I could see everything up close—the cats, the mice, the insects, and the big world outside, the one inhabited by Mine.

Life seemed to speed up after this. Mother taught Squirrel and me how to protect ourselves, when to hide and when to attack and, most important, how to find food and how to catch food. Finding food, I discovered, was easier than catching it—if there was a good garbage heap nearby. And the garbage heap at the edge of the Merrions' property was very good indeed. A dog never knew what he might discover there. All sorts of things for which I didn't have names then. But now I know what I was eating: bits of scrambled eggs, oatmeal, lettuce, crusts of bread, some things that did not taste very good and that upset my stomach, such as onions, and some things that tasted wonderful, such as cake and biscuits. One day when Squirrel and I were nosing through the garbage I found a whole chicken leg. I ate it without sharing.

By the time Mother introduced Squirrel and me to the garbage heap, the days were longer and much warmer, and the Merrions had returned to their house one morning and had not left it again for more than a few hours. Day after day they were there. They were interesting to watch, especially the young Merrions who shrieked and ran about, but Mother made Squirrel and me stay out of sight of the house, so exploring the yard became difficult.

The only creature on the property that seemed unconcerned by the Merrions was Mine. She crossed their yard by moonlight and by daylight, and finally one afternoon the Merrion child who was a girl saw her and let out a screech. Two days later, while Squirrel was following me on our out-of-sight route to the garbage heap, we were frightened by a blast so loud that it seemed I could feel the woods shake. We bolted toward the shed, but before we reached it we saw one of the Merrions' gardeners carrying a rifle, and nearby we saw Mine lying very still in a garden. Mother found us then and hustled us, unseen, into the shed where we spent the rest of the day.

Early the next morning Mother left the shed. I watched her trot away in the direction of the garbage. The day was very hot and very still and very quiet. We didn't hear any more blasts or see the man with the gun.

But Mother never came back.

At first we didn't know that Mother wouldn't return. Because Squirrel and I were bigger by then and could go off on our own, our mother sometimes left us for long periods of time. That day, the one that started when Mother trotted off, my sister and I hunted and played in the woods out of view of the Merrions. We visited the garbage heap too, and I tasted my first smoked turkey. The day grew hot; it was one of the hottest of the summer, and when the sun was at the highest point in the sky the Merrions went indoors and stayed there, in the big cool rooms. The woods became still, as if all the creatures that usually swooped and stalked and scurried and snuffled for food were hiding from the heat, like the Merrions. Even Squirrel and I stopped our playing, and we lay in the shade in the woods, waiting for Mother. At the end of the day, when the heat was starting to fade, we returned to the shed and waited some more.

Then we waited all night.

At the time when Squirrel and I were still too little to leave the wheelbarrow, but after the time my eyes and ears had opened, I had learned from watching the other shed creatures that things can change in an instant—*SNAP!* The swallow flew through the window and—*SNAP!*—the cat caught her in his jaws. A green insect perched on the window ledge and—*SNAP!*—a sparrow swallowed it. A snake slithered into the shed and—*SNAP!*—a mouse became lunch. Later, the Merrions' gardener took aim at Mine and—*SNAP!*—she was gone.

Something had happened to Mother. I don't know what it was, but I think she encountered a predator or a fast-moving car or an enemy—something that prevented her from returning to the shed. Otherwise, she wouldn't have left Squirrel and me when we were so young.

But, snap, Mother was gone and Squirrel and I were on our own.

At first I was like the surviving barn swallow. I looked for Mother and I waited for her. Then I looked less and less and waited less and less, and soon Mother simply was not part of my life. It was during this time—this time after

Mother had disappeared, and when Squirrel and I realized that we had learned enough of Mother's lessons to be able to fill our bellies with food and water and to stay away from dangerous creatures—that my sister and I were discovered.

Matthias Merrion found us.

It wasn't our fault. We were being careful as Mother had taught us to be, napping one afternoon in a good hiding place in the woods, and—*SNAP!*—suddenly there was Matthias, the middle Merrion child, the one who wanted a pet. He didn't see us at first, and we held as still as we possibly could. This was our mistake, though, because Matthias almost stepped on us. And then he cried, "Hey! I found puppies!"

Squirrel and I didn't waste a second. We leaped to our feet and ran directly to the shed where we huddled in our nest. But our legs weren't very long yet, and Matthias followed us easily. He opened the shed door and sat on the floor next to us. He talked to us. He said he wanted to be our friend.

And he did try very hard to be our friend. For many, many days we were his secret pets, and he brought us toys and chicken and tried to stroke our backs. Mother had taught us to fear humans, so we didn't like his hands much. But we liked his chicken. And sometimes, if our bellies weren't as full as they might have been, we allowed him to pet us in order to get the chicken reward. Eventually, when the days of summer were starting to grow shorter and the nights a bit cooler, Squirrel and I even allowed Matthias to pull us into his lap and to stroke our paws and whisper in our ears. Matthias was always gentle. And he almost always had chicken.

Our days on the Merrions' property were pleasant. We got along with the cats. We felt safer now that Mine was gone. (Her kits were gone too. They left after their mother was killed, and never came back.) And Matthias was nice to us.

But I never felt completely comfortable. At night I could hear coyotes in the hills. During the day I sometimes watched the Merrions from hidden places, watched them kill insects and set out traps for raccoons and put up fences to keep the deer out of their gardens. And then one afternoon I saw the man with the gun again. He walked all around the Merrions' yard and Mrs. Merrion trailed after him, saying, "They're nuisances. They're unsanitary and they don't belong here."

I didn't know what she was talking about, but I nudged Squirrel into the shed and made her spend the rest of the day there with me. The next morning, there was no sign of the man or the gun, so eventually Squirrel and I made our way to the garbage heap. Our bellies were rumbling. We hadn't eaten since the previous morning and Squirrel wanted to linger over the scraps of meat and pie and scrambled eggs, but we returned quickly to the safety of the shed. Maybe Matthias would visit us with fresh chicken. It was going to be a stay-in-the-shed day again.

That night, drowsing in our nest as darkness was falling, we heard a blast from the gun. Squirrel, half asleep, jerked to her feet with a loud yip and ran to a corner of the shed, braving the cats. We waited, motionless.

Nothing further happened that night. Squirrel came back to our nest and I stayed awake until dawn, watching and listening. At the first pink glow of the sun's rays, I stood and touched my nose to Squirrel's. This place was no longer safe for us.

It was time to leave.

2. CHARLIE

The day of RJ Elliot's eighth-grade graduation is hot, beastly hot. Every window in the gym is open wide, and flies and bees circle the families seated stickily on the metal folding chairs that have been arranged in rows on the varnished floor. Yesterday, Charlie Elliot was shooting hoops on this floor with three of his friends. Now he's sitting between his parents in the third row of seats, watching a fly ascend the back of Melinda Delroy's head. The girls who were in his fourth-grade class this year—those who have brothers or sisters in the eighth grade and are therefore attending the graduation ceremony—have made accordion fans out of their programs, which they're waving back and forth, back and forth in front of their faces, their necks, their arms. The boys pull their shirttails out, the women pat their faces with lavender-scented handkerchiefs, and some of the men remove their jackets, which they drape over the backs of the chairs.

The program hasn't started yet, so people keep approaching the Elliots, hands extended, faces grim.

"We're so sorry for your loss," they say. "Is there anything we can do? This must bring everything back for you."

Each kind word, each concerned face, causes Charlie's mother to weep again. She has wept and wept and wept these last seven months, wept so much that sties regularly bloom on her eyelids.

Charlie kicks at the back of Melinda's chair. He doesn't want to look at his father whose face is damp, even after wiping it with his big graying handkerchief. He wipes his entire face, from top to bottom, as if he's mopping away sweat. But everyone can see that Charlie's father is crying.

It's like the funeral all over again.

From the fourth row, Mrs. Hutchins, the mother of Charlie's friend Danny, leans forward and touches Charlie's mother on her shoulder. Mrs. Elliot dabs at her eyes, says nothing, but turns around just far enough to clasp Mrs. Hutchins's hands in feverish silence. Charlie looks away from the women toward the open door of the gym, the door leading to the playground. He can see Sunny sitting outside the doorway, can see her tail anyway. Faithful Sunny will wait until the ceremony is over, as long as it takes, in order to join her family and ride back to the farm in the bed of the pickup. This is her favorite way to ride—facing into the wind, ears blowing straight back, paying strict attention to whatever is ahead. RJ called her the Navigator.

The ceremony is supposed to begin now, right now.

The clock on the gym wall says 10:00 exactly, and Charlie wants things to get underway and then over with. When the clock says 10:02, the door from the east corridor of Jackson Elementary School suddenly opens into the gym— with a bang that startles Mrs. Elliot—and the principal strides across the gleaming floor to a podium that has been set up under one of the basketball nets. A thick black cord trails from the podium to a socket in the wall several feet away. The principal, a man named Mr. Nydick, who once praised RJ as the boy most likely to put Lindenfield on the map, smiles at the audience, then looks back toward the door he just banged open. And now the eighth-graders enter.

They file into the gym and seat themselves, as they re-hearsed the previous afternoon, in the two rows of chairs that face the audience. Eighteen chairs, seventeen gradu-ates. The empty chair is RJ's.

Charlie allows his gaze to travel from the empty chair to Mr. Nydick's face, now solemn, out the door to Sunny, who has shifted her position and is dozing in the sun, and beyond to the heartbreakingly blue sky and the tail of a kite.

Charlie wishes to be anywhere other than at the grad-uation of his dead brother.

Lindenfield is the smallest town in Monroe County. A total of eighty-nine students in grades K through eight attend

14

Jackson Elementary School on Dean Avenue, which is the main road in town. Also on Dean are the public library, the post office, the dime store, the movie theater, two churches, a new Chinese restaurant (considered extremely foreign and somewhat suspect), the diner in which Charlie and RJ once ate an entire banana bomb (a concoction twice the size of a banana split), a hardware store, and the store Charlie calls the Everything Else Store because it sells everything not sold in the other stores, from underwear to lamps. On the county road leading out of town are a feed store, a grocery store, and two gas stations.

People who are born in Lindenfield tend to stay there. Charlie's parents were born in Lindenfield and they attended Jackson Elementary. Since his first day in kindergarten, Charlie has marveled at the thought that he might be lying on the very same resting mat his father used (the mat looks—and smells—old enough for that) or holding in his hands a library book his mother once borrowed. When he started second grade, he savored the fact that his teacher, Mrs. Shucard, had taught not only RJ, but both Mr. and Mrs. Elliot.

Mr. Nydick is speaking now, talking about each of the graduates in turn. He mentions Jean Anne's talent for home economics and Howard's prowess on the Little League field and the lovely rhyming poetry Emily writes, and he's getting closer and closer to RJ's chair. Hugh Delroy is sitting next to the empty chair, and after Mr. Nydick reminds the audience of the time Hugh wrote a letter to the editor of the *Lindenfield Journal* protesting the rising cost of school lunches, he glances at the chair and his speech crawls to a halt.

Mr. Nydick removes his glasses and polishes them on his handkerchief, which he slips back in his pocket. He turns from the graduates to the audience, and Charlie decides that without the glasses his principal looks a little like a possum.

"The students you see here before you," says Mr. Nydick, "have reached many milestones during their years at Jackson. Together they have learned to read, appeared in plays and pageants, and welcomed their parents on Visiting Days. They've celebrated birthdays and holidays, bid farewell to retiring teachers, and marked the births of sisters and brothers, many of whom are here today. And in September they will become members of the freshman class at Monroe County High School.

"They began this year, their final year at Jackson, as a class of eighteen students. And now," Mr. Nydick takes the pause Charlie knew was coming, "now they are a class of seventeen. In November, we lost RJ Elliot."

Mrs. Elliot reaches across Charlie and takes her husband's hand.

"RJ," Mr. Nydick continues, "was an outstanding student and a fine member of our community. We feel his presence every bit as much today as we did before we lost him."

Charlie notes that nobody can admit that RJ died. He has simply become lost, which Charlie supposes is true in some way, because where is he? Charlie remembers seeing him lying on the ground under the fir tree, but not any time after that, even though Charlie ran for his mother and later returned to the tree and waited with her for the ambulance to arrive.

The day RJ died was not remarkable in any way. Charlie has read lots and lots of books and often, he has noticed, the day on which a character dies is, ironically, the only sunny day in a string of cloudy ones, or memorable because it's someone's birthday or a holiday. But the November day that turned out to be RJ's last was not particularly sunny or cloudy or warm or cool. And it was not a holiday or anything special. The school bus had deposited Charlie and RJ, as usual, at the end of the lane leading to their farm that afternoon and they had been greeted joyously by Sunny as they approached the house. Their mother had had cake waiting for them in the kitchen and had asked how much homework they had, and when they convinced her that they could do it after dinner, they had left the house in a hurry. RJ had taken off with Sunny at his heels—as usual—and Charlie had crossed the yard to the barn. The barn, complete with stalls and a haymow, had once been home to a number of cows and one donkey, but was now a work space and the office for Mr. Elliot's painting business and Mrs. Elliot's egg-selling business. And it was here that Charlie had made his first kite. The day before, he had completed the last step. He had painted a griffin on it, carefully copying the creature from the *GRI* page in the encyclopedia, and now the paint was dry, and Charlie left the barn, eager to test his kite.

He ran past the henhouse, past the remains of the vegetable garden, and through the overgrown field, allowing the wind to jerk the kite aloft. Three times it crashed to the ground, and Charlie patiently rescued it and sent it aloft again. At last it sailed steadily, high above, flapping satisfyingly, and Charlie let out a shout, hoping RJ would see his masterpiece, especially since he had doubted Charlie's kite-building abilities. But now here was the kite with its tail smacking behind, tied with rags like the tails of kites Charlie had seen in picture books, and RJ didn't answer Charlie's call, and that was a disappointment. Charlie was alone in his triumph.

Charlie ran and ran, reeling the kite in, then letting the spool unwind, and suddenly he realized he had let out too much string and far, far ahead he could see the kite wobble and dive. He stopped to catch his breath, bent over, hands on his knees. When he straightened up he began to walk through the field, following the string, winding it on the spool as he went, wondering where his kite had landed. He was approaching the fir trees behind the barn when he heard the sound of branches breaking and a cry and then a heavy, dull thud like someone dropping a sack of grain. Sunny began to bark and Charlie quickened his pace, because he recognized Sunny's bark of alarm. He ran until he reached the trees, and there was RJ lying on the ground, Sunny at his side.

"RJ!" Charlie had shouted. "RJ!"

RJ was motionless. One arm was above his head as if he were about to catch a ball; his legs were bent as if he were running.

Later when people in Lindenfield spoke of the accident they always pointed out RJ's heroism, but sometimes they also remembered to mention the speed with which Charlie ran to the house to get help. Mrs. Elliot, busy making dinner, had called the ambulance and then run back to the fir trees, back to where Sunny was now lying next to RJ, whimpering, her head nestled on his chest. The ambulance had arrived in fifteen minutes, but by then RJ had already drawn his last breath. He was taken to the hospital, but even before he was lifted onto the stretcher he was gone—lost or dead.

"...our hero," Mr. Nydick was now saying. "For RJ Elliot was a true hero, a boy revered by his peers and admired by adults, an outstanding student and athlete, whose last act was a good deed for his brother. RJ was brave, selfless, smart, and true."

Charlie can't raise his head. His eyes are on the floor. He remembers RJ spending Saturdays helping out old Mr. Hanna on the neighboring property, RJ leading Lindenfield's Little League team to victory, RJ, who would have graduated first in his class, winning the county math prize. He also remembers RJ and Hugh trying out cigarettes in the haymow, and RJ sneaking out his window after the Elliots had gone to bed, and RJ at age twelve driving Mr. Elliot's truck into the wall of the barn, all things to which Charlie had been forcibly sworn to secrecy.

"Charlie," Mrs. Elliot whispers. "Get ready."

Charlie focuses on Mr. Nydick. "So even though we lost RJ last autumn," Mr. Nydick is saying, "we will remember him forever as a treasured student, classmate, son, brother, and friend. I would now like to award RJ's diploma in memoriam. Here to accept it is his brother, Charlie."

For the last few weeks, Charlie has worried about this walk from his seat in the audience to the podium, worried that he will somehow get it wrong, and now he finds that he can't cover the distance fast enough. He reaches Mr. Nydick in a matter of seconds, says "Thank you" when he's handed the diploma, and hightails it back to his chair, handing the diploma to his mother on the way.

Ten minutes later the ceremony is over. The audience

rises to their feet as the afternoon heat rolls through the windows in waves. The seventeen graduates let out cheers, the girls hug, the boys slap hands.

A small crowd surrounds the Elliots. Since Mrs. Elliot is crying, Mrs. Delroy puts her arms around her. Mr. Delroy pats Charlie on the back. "Proud of your brother, aren't you?" he says. And someone else says, "His last act. Going after your kite."

Charlie squirms away from the crowd. He's the first to leave the gym and he squats in the dusty yard beside Sunny. He can't help but think, as he fondles Sunny's silky ears, that RJ was the one who named Sunny; that Sunny had, in fact, been RJ's dog.

3. HENRY

What I Would Like For Christmas

1. Treasore Island

2. biagraphy of Jackie Robinson

3. any Hardy Boys books I don't have, you can check my bookshelfs the books are in number order

4. dog

5. oil pants

6. baseball players autagraph any one will be fine

7. doghouse

8. sketchpad

9. everything for a dog

I hope this isn't asking for too much. It isn't even ten things.

By Henry

Henry read through the Christmas list. He had written it two years earlier, when he was nine. Even though the list was now completely outdated—and even though he found the spelling errors highly embarrassing—he had saved the list because he thought it was clever. And every so often he liked to take the list out of his desk drawer and marvel at it. He thought that leading off with *Treasure Island* had been especially clever. He had known that the request for a classic would appeal to his parents, both of whom were librarians. Not that Henry didn't like to read. Reading had been his main hobby two years ago, and it was his main hobby now (followed by art and the study of baseball players), and he really had wanted to read *Treasure Island*. But mostly he had needed to grab his parents' attention, wanted to be certain they'd read the rest of the list.

Henry thought that burying his request for a dog after several seemingly more important items (all books) was also very clever. Number 4—*dog*—had actually been the sole purpose for drawing up the list. And it was the main reason Henry had saved the list. He had wanted a dog for as long as he could remember, and two years ago was the first time he had included the request in a Christmas list. It hadn't worked, though. He had received items 1, 2, 3, 5, 6, and 8, but not the dog, the doghouse, or anything else for a dog.

Henry threw his covers back. He had awakened long before his alarm clock rang and had decided to use the extra time to write a new Christmas list, even if it *was* only October and technically too early for such things. However, he had thought and thought and couldn't come up with anything he truly wanted, other than a dog.

Henry set the old list on his bedside table. He turned around, knelt on his pillow, raised the window shade, and peered across the street at Matthew's house, which already had the feel of an abandoned tree fort. It was funny, Henry thought, how you could just look at a house and know whether anyone lived in it. Matthew's family had moved out the previous afternoon—less than one day ago—and overnight the house had acquired an air of emptiness. And aloneness.

"Stupid Matthew," Henry muttered.

Matthew had been Henry's best friend.

A squeaking sound from the corner of the room caused Henry to turn around again. Hamlet had begun to run frantically on the wheel in his cage. His feet moved so fast that Henry couldn't see them. Hamlet the hamster was what Henry's parents had gotten him the first time he had come right out and asked for a dog. Hamlet's cage mate, Carlos Beltran, was what they had gotten him the second time he had asked for a dog. Last spring when he had again asked for a dog, his parents had taken him to the shelter and told him to choose a cat, which he had done, and that was how Amelia Earhart had joined the family.

Henry turned back to the window and muttered "Stupid Matthew" again. Without Matthew, Henry had no one to walk to school with. He had no one to discuss baseball players with, no one to prowl the stacks of the libraries with, and no one to do his sixth-grade homework with. Matthew had been Henry's best friend and his only friend. Having Matthew right across the street had been so convenient that Henry had never bothered to make any other friends. What was the point?

Henry glanced at his Christmas list, the new one. He had carefully written the numbers 1 through 5 down the left-hand side of the paper, but the rest of the page was blank. He looked at the old list again, and then he got an idea. He drew a line through items 1, 2, 3, 5, 6, and 8. There. That should do it. Only numbers 4, 7, and 9 were left. Henry hoped he was making his point. He threw away the useless new list and folded the old one into quarters.

Henry got dressed and slouched his way downstairs to the kitchen. His parents were already seated at the table.

"Hi," said Henry dolefully. He slid into his chair, rested

his head against his palm, and with the other hand, extended the folded piece of paper. "Here."

"What's this?" asked his mother.

"My Christmas list. I was feeling sad this morning," said Henry. "About Matthew and everything. So I thought I could make myself feel better by looking forward to Christmas."

"Very practical," commented his father.

"I'll put the list right over here," said his mother, and she placed it, still folded, on top of a pile of unopened mail that occupied one end of the kitchen counter.

"You know," said Henry, "one thing every kid needs is a best friend."

"True," agreed his father.

"And I was thinking that a best friend doesn't have to be a kid. A best friend could be a parent or a grandparent or, I don't know, a dog."

"Pets make wonderful friends," said his mother.

"They sure do. Especially *dogs*," said Henry.

"Who are you going to walk to school with today?" asked Henry's father.

Henry slumped in his chair. "I don't know. It really is sad, not having a best friend anymore."

"What about Owen?" asked his mother.

"Who's Owen?"

"Owen *Hen*derson," said his mother with some surprise. Henry's mother was the librarian at Henry's school, as well as the vice principal, and she knew practically every kid in town. "He lives right down the street. On the corner of Mountain View."

"Oh, him." Henry shrugged. "I don't know. I don't think Owen and I have anything in common."

There were good things and bad things about living in a town as small as Claremont, which was where Henry had lived his entire life. Claremont was so teeny that Henry could walk from one end of it to the other (from the elementary school to the grocery store) in fifteen minutes, if he didn't stop to peer in the windows of any of the stores in between. And he and most of the kids in town were allowed to roam around on their own as long as they looked carefully before they crossed the street. These were two good things about small-town life.

On weekends and after school, Henry and Matthew had explored every inch of Claremont. They knew the location of each store and business on Nassau Street. They knew the order in which the side streets crossed Nassau, each one beginning and ending several blocks away at the edge of the woods, the woods then creeping up the mountains that formed the valley in which Claremont lay. Henry had always liked the idea that, just by walking the length of his own road, Tinker Lane, he could travel from a forest and a mountain across Nassau to another forest and another mountain. He felt that he lived in a town and the country all at the same time.

On the other hand, simply because Claremont was so small, Henry felt that the possibility of his making friends other than Matthew was rather limited. Henry's three interests—reading, art, and baseball players—had been shared by Matthew, but he didn't think they were shared by the other boys in town, at least not in that particular combination. Henry had spent a certain amount of time observing his classmates and he knew that most of them, the boys especially, were far more interested in playing baseball than in learning facts about baseball players. And he didn't know any other kid, boy or girl, apart from Matthew, who was methodically reading his way through the fiction section of both libraries (school and public) and who had a favorite volume of the encyclopedia. (Henry's was *D*, since it included so much information on dogs, but he also liked *T* because of its fascinating photo of the damage caused by an F-5 tornado. Matthew's was *R* because of Jackie Robinson. He didn't have a second favorite.)

"Well, what about the other boys in your grade?" Henry's mother now asked him.

Henry shrugged again. "It's okay. I'm going to walk by myself. I've done it before. On the days Matthew was absent."

Amelia Earhart ambled into the kitchen then. She came to a stop in the exact center of the room and sat down, curling her tail around her front feet.

"Did you know," said Henry, "that a cat's digestive system—"

Henry's father held up one hand. "Is this breakfast table material?" he asked.

"No," admitted Henry. "But it's really interesting. Cats can digest—"

"Henry," said his mother.

"Okay. Dad?"

"Yes?"

"Did that person return *All-of-a-Kind Family* yet?"

"What person?"

"Whoever checked it out." Henry didn't particularly want to read *All-of-a-Kind Family*, but it was the only book by a *T* author in the fiction section of the children's room at the public library (where Henry's father was the head librarian) that Henry hadn't read yet, and he didn't want to go on to *U* without completing *T* first. Henry had set out to read everything in the children's room three years earlier. Now that he was eleven, a lot of the books were too babyish for him, but he wasn't ready to give up on his project. He was too close to the end.

"I'll check today," said his father.

"If it's back, could you bring it home with you? Please?" asked Henry.

Henry's father pulled a pad of paper from his pocket and wrote a note on it. "If it isn't in, what should I bring you?"

"Oh, I guess just any book about a dog would do." Henry paused, then added, "As long as the author's last name begins with *A*, *B*, *C*, *D*, *E*, *F*, *G*, *H*, *I*, *J*, *K*, *L*, *M*, *N*, *O*, *P*, *Q*, *R*, *S*, or *T*. Nothing after *T*."

Henry's parents looked at each other and sighed. "You're sure you don't want to—" his father started to ask.

Henry interrupted him. "Nope. It's my rule." He looked at his watch and pushed his chair back from the table in a hurry. If he was going to leave the house before his parents did, he would have to hurry. In a town as small as Claremont, most people, Henry's parents among them, could walk to work, and Henry was not about to trail after his mother all the way to school just because Matthew was gone.

Henry put on his backpack, which weighed more than usual since he had decided to bring along activities so he could entertain himself during recess. He had packed his current sketch pad, three books (it was good to have a choice of reading material), and a stack of baseball cards. He crossed his lawn, stopped, and stared at Matthew's house with its forlorn, left-behind look. He threw a stone at the living room window, but it landed harmlessly in the middle of the yard.

"Stupid Matthew."

Henry set off down the street. At his back were the woods and the yellow DEAD END sign. He thought that placing a DEAD END sign at the dead end itself was pointless, since you could see the dead end right there where the road came to a complete stop and the forest began. Ahead of him was the corner of Aspen Avenue, then the corner of Mountain View, then Morton Road, then Nassau, and beyond Nassau, three more intersections, and then another pointless DEAD END sign at the base of the mountain on the far side of Claremont.

Henry paid attention to the houses on Tinker Lane as he passed by. He realized that he barely knew anything about the people who lived in them. To his left was the large Victorian home with the wide white porch and the window frames painted in shades of lavender and gray. Over the years, he and Matthew had made up so many stories about the little old lady who lived there that now he couldn't remember what they had invented and what he might have heard his parents say. *A little old lady who almost never comes outside,* he thought. Matthew had said the word for a person like that was *recluse*. Henry stopped in front of the house and took a good look at it. It was enormous. Did just one person truly live there all by herself? He noted that in the yard on both sides of the house bird feeders hung from the oak trees. He saw a birdhouse nailed to a wooden post and a birdbath in a small garden, the basin now filled with autumn leaves.

Henry moved on. He crossed Aspen and started down the next block. A noisy group of kids was ahead of him, on the other side of Mountain View. They poked one another and laughed and shouted and jumped in the leaves piled along the sidewalk. One of the kids was Owen, Henry thought, and another was Antony, who was in Henry's grade. Antony, he now recalled, had four brothers and sisters.

Henry watched the short yellow school bus pull up in front of a tidy white house, and he stopped walking for a moment. The short bus was transportation for kids in the classroom at the end of the south wing of his school, the room called the Learning Center. The door of the house opened now and a woman pushed a wheelchair through it and down a ramp toward the driveway. A small girl sat in the wheelchair. The door of the house opened a second time and a boy ran down the ramp and joined the group of kids ahead of Henry. The boy was Mackey Brannigan, who was also in Henry's grade. How many times, Henry wondered, had he and Matthew walked down Tinker Lane lost in their world of baseball players and books and

32

paid no attention to the old lady's house or the short bus or Antony and Owen and Mackey?

The bus pulled away from the curb, the kids crossed Morton and turned the corner onto Nassau Street, and Henry continued down Tinker by himself.

If I had a dog, he thought, *I would name him Buddy.*

4. BONE

The shed had been a good home for Squirrel and me. It had been warm in the cool weather, it had sheltered us from rain, and it had hidden us from the Merrions. But it couldn't protect us from everything. The yipping coyotes reminded me of that. And the man with the gun reminded me of that. Early the morning after Squirrel and I were frightened by the second blast from the gun, I rose from our bed on the floor. I looked around the shed; looked at the nesting boxes on the far wall, sleepy cat eyes peering through some of the holes; looked at the abandoned barn swallow nest; looked at the open window and beyond to the branches of a birch tree.

Squirrel had been stretched out on the burlap sacks, breathing deeply, but when she felt me get to my feet, she opened her eyes. She sat up, and I touched my nose to hers. I was going to leave our home, but I couldn't leave my sister.

I slipped through the door. The other creatures in the shed were starting to stir, and several of them blinked at me, but most paid no attention. Squirrel and I lived in a separate dog world and were of little interest to the cats and mice and insects. I began to trot along the bushes at the edge of the Merrions' yard, but I stopped every so often to glance back at the shed. The first time I did so I saw only the open door. The second time, I saw Squirrel's snout poking through the door. The third time, I saw Squirrel standing in front of the shed. And the fourth time, I saw that Squirrel was following me. I had passed the garbage pile by then, heading into new territory. When Squirrel caught up with me, we trotted along side by side for a while. Every now and then Squirrel would turn to give me a lick. We bounced through the woods, the rising sun warming our backs.

That day was like no other Squirrel and I had experienced. Gone were our familiar landmarks. Gone was the garbage pile. Gone were the shed cats and Matthias and the man with the gun. Gone was everything, good and bad, that we had known. We made our way through woods that were just like our own and at the same time entirely different. Here were familiar things—ferns and saplings and bramble bushes, chipmunks and garden snakes and grasshoppers, blue jays and crows and chickadees. But we had no idea what we would find over a rise or across a stream or beyond a boulder.

At first we felt frisky. We chased each other. We played

in a brook. I pounced on a butterfly. By the time the shadows were growing longer, though; by the time the air, which had warmed as the sun had risen, was becoming cooler again, our stomachs were rumbling with hunger. And I didn't know where to find food. We would need to hunt.

I walked ahead of Squirrel now, but my steps were slower than when I had left the shed. I was on the lookout for rodents when suddenly the trees ended and my sister and I found ourselves at the edge of a wide field. A tractor sat at one end of the field, and from somewhere not too far away came a sound that I knew meant cars. Squirrel and I had heard the Merrions' car many times on the lane to their house. When we were old enough to roam from the shed, we had discovered a road much bigger than their lane with many more cars. The sound I heard now was of lots of cars traveling very fast.

I perked up my ears and listened for other sounds. Then I put my nose in the air and sniffed. Squirrel and I needed a meal—quickly. The field seemed like a good place for rodents, so I set off through it and soon enough I caught the scent of rabbit. But a long chase through the field after a very fast bunny led not to a meal but to the busy road and the cars.

I didn't like the road and neither did Squirrel. Cars and trucks bore down on us in rushes of hot wind, blowing dust in our eyes. Squirrel turned back toward the field in a hurry, but now I caught the scent of something else, something better than bunny.

Chicken.

I could smell chicken nearby.

My mouth watered.

But where was the chicken? I sat up straight, ignoring the rushing traffic, and stuck my snout in the air again. I sniffed and sniffed and sniffed, my nose twitching. And suddenly I knew exactly where the chicken was. Across the highway I could see a paper bag on its side. My nose told me that chicken was in that bag.

I stood poised by the edge of the road as car after truck zoomed by, and I waited for my opportunity to run. I was still waiting when I heard Squirrel let out a sharp bark. Before I could turn to her I felt hands, human hands like those belonging to Matthias, scoop me up in the air. I twisted around and found myself looking into the face of a man who was breathing very hard. I swiveled my head around and saw that Squirrel had been scooped up by a woman. By the side of the road a little distance away, a car was idling. And far, far across the road was the chicken, its scent still easing its way to me on the wind.

The woman who was holding my sister said, "Look, they're just puppies. What are they doing way out here?"

The man put his face very close to mine and said in a deep voice that was like Mother's warning growl, "You

guys could have gotten yourselves killed. This is a dangerous highway."

"Well, honey, they don't know any better," replied the
woman. "They're little. They must have gotten lost."

That was when the man said, "Do they have any col-
lars or tags?" and he began to explore my neck with fingers that were not gentle like Matthias's.

Once, not long after Mother had decided that Squirrel
and I could explore the woods on our own, we had come
across a pond and—*SNAP!*—a fierce turtle had reached
around with his long neck and nearly clamped his jaws on
my front paw. We were careful around turtles after that.

Now I snapped at the man like the turtle had snapped at
me. "Hey!" he shouted. "You little brat! Don't do that again."
He gave me a shake and I could feel my teeth rattle. I looked
at Squirrel, who was squirming in the woman's hands. The
more my sister squirmed, the tighter the woman held her
until finally Squirrel let out a squeak.

I tried to bite the man again, but he tucked me under
one arm, opened the door of the car that was stopped by
the side of the road, and stuck me in the back. The woman
stuck Squirrel in next to me. Then they climbed into the
front seat.

"What are we going to do with them?" asked the man.

"Keep them!" exclaimed the woman. "They're cute."

Before I knew it, my sister and I were speeding

down the road, getting farther and farther away from the chicken.

The man and the woman were named George and Marcy. I think that they *wanted* to want Squirrel and me, but that they didn't really like animals very much. Also, we were too much trouble. Squirrel got sick in their car, and as soon as Marcy carried her inside their house, she peed on the floor. George shouted, "*Bad* dog!" then in a very loud voice and tossed her out the front door. He brought her back inside, though, and Marcy put us in the kitchen and then I made a puddle on the floor, and Squirrel pooped in a corner.

"Well, it's pretty clear that they've never lived in a house," said George.

He lifted the lid on the garbage pail in order to throw away a handful of wet paper towels, and that was when I smelled something just as good as chicken—turkey. Plus eggs and cookies and bread and bologna. In a flash, I darted to the pail and knocked it over, and Squirrel and I snatched at the spilled food and swallowed what we could grab without bothering to chew it. We retreated, growling, under the table, and this time Marcy yelled, "Bad dogs!"

We fell asleep beneath the table.

When we woke up later that night, Marcy was setting my sister and me in a large box lined with newspapers. We didn't like the box. And we needed to pee. We whined and howled, but Marcy didn't take us out of the box. Instead she picked us up, box and all, carried us into a room with no windows, and set the box on the floor. This was the darkest space I had ever been in. I couldn't see a speck of moonlight. I couldn't hear a single sound either—no cats purring or owls calling or even coyotes yipping. Nothing. There was only silence and the deep black.

Squirrel and I had to pee in our sleeping place. We didn't have a choice.

I fell asleep at last. When I awoke, the night was over. A door had opened into our room and flooded it with light from a window across a hallway. I saw Squirrel next to me. And I saw a hand on her back. I leaped forward and bit the hand. Marcy slapped me on my nose. I yelped.

I could hear George call, "What is it?"

"The tan puppy just bit me!" said Marcy.

"Okay," replied George. "That does it. Those dogs go today."

Marcy said no, but as soon as she left the house, George put on a pair of gloves, found a box that was smaller than the one we had spent the night in, and slammed it onto the floor of the kitchen. He did these things in silence, except for the slamming, and he moved very fast and very heavily. Squirrel and I were under the kitchen table and we had backed up against the wall, as far from George as we could get, but his hands came after us anyway. He shoved aside a chair and grabbed me by the scruff of my neck. He ignored me when I tried to whip around like the snapping turtle again and bite his gloved hand, and he stuffed me into the new box. He stuffed Squirrel in next, and then he carried the box a little distance and tossed it onto something that caused us to land with a bounce. I heard the sound of a car starting, and soon Squirrel and I were on another ride. When we whimpered, George told us to shut *up* and he whacked the box. After that, we didn't make any noise.

We rode in the car for a short time and presently it slowed down and the top of our box was ripped open. The glove reached in and grabbed me by my neck, and in the next instant I was sailing through the air. I landed on something hard, smashing my nose, but I didn't stop to lick at the blood. I turned around, looking for Squirrel, and there she was sailing through the air too. Before she had even landed, George's car sped up. It zoomed away, making a great deal of noise.

I heard a cracking sound when my sister hit the pavement, but she didn't yelp or whimper, just staggered onto her hind legs before flopping down again. I stood up. I wanted to run to her, but one of my front paws hurt so much that at first I couldn't put any weight on it. I sat for a moment, shaking and panting.

Squirrel and I had landed on a patch of asphalt wider than any road I had seen. It was wider than a stream, wider even than the Merrions' yard. And it was lined with rows and rows and rows of stopped cars. Beyond the cars was an enormous building, and people were going in and out of it through tall glass doors.

I tried once again to stand up, and this time I was able to put weight on all of my legs. I began to limp toward Squirrel and had almost reached her when I heard someone exclaim, "Hey, did you see that? Someone threw those puppies out of a car!"

Then another voice said, "Are they all right?"

Two women were walking along one of the rows of cars. They were carrying large bags made of paper. Now they began to run toward Squirrel and me. When they reached us they set the bags on the ground and knelt down.

"Oh, my goodness," one of them said. This woman had hair so long that it tumbled over her shoulders and halfway down her back. Also, the middle part of her was fat but the rest was not.

"I think they're okay," said the other woman. This second woman was wearing a hat and it was as blue as a jay's feather.

"Look how cute this one is," said the woman with the long hair. "Look at her brown eyes. I wonder if she's a golden retriever." She held her hand out toward me. "I always wanted a puppy. I'm going to take the tan one home."

"But what about the spotted one?"

The woman paused. "I don't think I can manage two dogs. And the other one isn't as cute. I'll just take this one." She stretched her hand even closer to me, and held it steady. I sniffed it. "Anyway, someone else will come along soon and find the spotted dog. That's why that guy dumped them at the mall, you know."

The woman with the long hair sat down on the asphalt. She talked softly to me, like Matthias used to do. After I had sniffed her hand again she put it on my back and stroked me. She kept whispering and stroking, whispering and stroking. And then she picked me up. I squirmed, and she held me tightly but not too tightly and said, "You'll be okay. You'll be okay." She wiped my bloody snout with a tissue.

The woman with the hat picked up all the bags, and the woman with the long hair held me firmly in her arms, and they began to walk away from my sister. After a while they stopped walking and the woman with the hat opened the door of a car. She put the bags inside while the woman with the long hair slid into a seat and settled me in her lap, in front of the part of her that was so fat. She never stopped talking to me in her low voice, murmuring that I was a good girl (she had a surprise coming) and that I was brave and strong and that she was going to take me to a vet. (I didn't know then what a vet was.) She patted me, and I didn't feel the need to bite her, so she kept patting and I kept my teeth to myself.

The woman with the hat started the car and drove it slowly along the asphalt. I was beginning to feel sleepy, but suddenly I stood up on my hind legs, put my front paws against the window, and looked outside. We were passing my sister. She was sitting where she had landed, gazing around at the cars and holding one of her front feet off the ground.

I barked once, loudly, and the woman with the long hair settled me in her lap again. She turned to the other woman. "Wait until Thad sees what I've brought home."

The woman with the hat said, "A puppy *and* a baby. You guys are going to be busy."

My eyes started to close and presently I fell asleep. I dreamed of walking nose to nose through the woods with Squirrel, but later the dream became unpleasant because I could see my sister sitting all by herself on the asphalt, wondering what to do next.

5. CHARLIE

In summertime, the Elliots' farm is a dry and dusty centerpiece in the flatlands surrounding Lindenfield. Charlie watches it grow larger, seeming to rise up out of the scorched earth, as his father steers the pickup along their lane. Sunny the Navigator sits on a sack of chicken feed in the back of the truck, facing just slightly to the left of the cab so that she can see where the truck is headed. Charlie sits next to her, his arms wrapped around her, the wind whipping his hair and drying the perspiration that trickles from his forehead.

Charlie appreciates this view of the farm and gazes at it with as much concentration as Sunny when she gazes at squirrels or people or sometimes nothing. From this distance it looks like the toy farm Charlie and RJ played with when they were little. There's the white house with the black shutters and the porch meandering from one side around the front to the other side; the red barn with straw spilling out of the haymow; the silo; the vegetable garden; the oak tree by the house; the grove of fir trees behind the barn; the lane leading from the county road to the side of the house. When Charlie used to play with the toy farm he would set it up to resemble his own farm as closely as possible, and he always placed four figures somewhere among the wooden buildings and trees. The set had come with a mother, a father, a boy, and a girl, but Charlie had discarded the girl figure and made a second brother by cutting a picture of a boy out of the Sears catalog and gluing it to a piece of cardboard.

Mr. Elliot slows the truck and parks it in front of the house. He and Charlie's mother climb out of the cab, stepping carefully to avoid the dust that rises around their polished shoes. Charlie can't wait to change his clothes.

"Well," says Charlie's father in an exceptionally cheerful tone of voice, "summer vacation is officially here. What do you think, Charlie?"

Charlie shrugs. As far as he's concerned, today is just another day without RJ. And now the entire summer—without RJ—yawns ahead. Charlie looks at his parents and realizes that his father is waiting for an answer. "Maybe I'll take Sunny for a walk in the woods," he says.

Inside the Elliots' cool house, shades drawn to shoo away the heat, Charlie climbs the stairs to his bedroom and changes into a pair of jeans and a striped T-shirt, both purchased at the Everything Else Store. He starts for the stairs, then turns back to his room. It's always a good idea to take a book along on one of his hikes with Sunny. He never knows when he might have a few minutes for reading. A little-known fact is that although Charlie was four years younger than RJ, he had read many more of the books in the Jackson Elementary School library than his brother had. Charlie reads, reads, reads, impressing the librarian. But somehow reading is not as noticeable as winning prizes or saving the day on the Little League field.

In the kitchen, Charlie slaps together a peanut butter and jelly sandwich, wraps it in wax paper, and drops it, an apple, and *Lassie Come-Home* in his knapsack.

"Come on, girl!" he says, patting his knee, and Sunny, who was resting in a corner of the kitchen, leaps to her feet, wide awake in an instant.

Charlie wonders if Sunny misses RJ. It's hard to tell with dogs.

He kicks the screen door open with his foot (his parents are not around to see this), and calls, "Sunny and I are going now!"

"Have fun," his father says from the living room. His voice sounds strangled.

Charlie lopes across the yard in the direction of the barn, and of the fir trees that he still has trouble looking at. Sunny runs ahead, plumed tail held high. She has a coat of reddish hair with a white fringe—her feathers—on the backs of her legs, and a long, delicate nose, which RJ called her snout, but *snout* is far too crude a word, Charlie thinks, for such a noble nose. Maybe Sunny is a collie, maybe a shepherd of some kind; probably both, plus a few other things.

Before they reach the barn, Charlie changes his mind about their route and veers to the left, whistling for Sunny. Sunny alters her course and soon she's running along in front of Charlie again. If they're heading southwest, they must be going to Mr. Hanna's.

Mr. Hanna's property borders the Elliots' so even though his house sits almost a mile from theirs, he's Charlie's neighbor. Charlie hasn't been by in several weeks, though, and today he notices, as he and Sunny make their way across a scraggly field, that the house is badly in need of painting and that the gardens, the ones his wife once tended so carefully, are now choked with weeds.

He knocks on Mr. Hanna's door. "Hello?" he calls. And he has to call twice more since Mr. Hanna is growing deaf.

"Charlie? Is that you?" he says at last. "Come on in."

Charlie holds the door open for Sunny and they find Mr. Hanna in his kitchen. He's cleaning his guns. Charlie stops just short of grimacing.

"Well, well. Charlie! And my Sunny. To what do I owe this honor?" Before Charlie can answer, Mr. Hanna puts his rifle down and says, "Oh. Was today the graduation?" He reaches for Sunny and strokes her silky ears.

Charlie nods.

"I see," says Mr. Hanna.

"What are you doing with the guns?" asks Charlie. "It's not hunting season."

"Gophers," is Mr. Hanna's reply.

"But why do you have to *shoot* them?"

Mr. Hanna doesn't answer and Charlie doesn't know whether he didn't hear or didn't want to hear, but he lets the subject drop. He thinks guns should never have been invented, that hunting is wrong, and that hunting season should be outlawed—unpopular opinions around Lindenfield—but he likes Mr. Hanna.

"How's your mother?" asks Mr. Hanna.

"Sad."

"I suppose today was a hard day. Brought everything back, did it?"

"Yeah. We got his diploma."

Mr. Hanna gazes out the window. "Uh-huh."

Charlie isn't sure how to phrase what he wants to ask. Finally, he says, "I noticed that your gardens are sort of weedy. And also that the porch could use some paint. The thing is, Dad has some extra cans of paint in the barn—left over from working at the Millers'—and he said I could have them. What I was wondering is if you need anyone to do some chores around here. I don't have a job this summer."

Charlie would be happy to do the work for free, but he doesn't want to hurt Mr. Hanna's pride.

Mr. Hanna frowns, then grins and says, "Well, you got yourself a job now, boy." He doesn't look at Charlie, though. Instead he gives Sunny another pat. Then he says to her, "Shake."

Sunny obediently offers her paw.

"Show me the rest of her tricks," says Mr. Hanna, and Charlie puts Sunny through her paces, a routine patiently taught to her by RJ.

Sit. Sit pretty. Roll over. Dance. Sing.

At the command to sing, Sunny throws her head back and howls, and Mr. Hanna laughs.

"Care to stay for lunch?" asks Mr. Hanna as Charlie is rising to his feet.

Charlie pats his knapsack. "Thanks. I got lunch in here."

"You and Sunny off on a tromp, then?"

"Yes, sir."

"When would you like to start your job?"

"Tomorrow?"

"Deal. Come at ten, bring that paint, and I'll throw lunch into the bargain."

Charlie and Sunny leave the field behind and enter the woods. These woods are not on the Elliots' land, nor on Mr. Hanna's, but Charlie knows them as well as he knows any part of his own property. He knows where the birch

50

grove is, and the flat rock that's big enough to stretch out on (a good place for reading, even if it is as hard as, well, a rock), and the tiny walled-off cemetery belonging to some long-ago and forgotten family, and the twists and turns of the stream that feeds into the pond at Mr. Hanna's.

Charlie once asked Mr. Hanna how far the stream went and Mr. Hanna suggested that he and RJ follow it, but RJ never had enough time and Charlie didn't want to do it alone.

One of the many good things about Mr. Hanna is that he has never asked Charlie about the kite or the tree or any of the details about the afternoon RJ died. Other adults want the details, which they mostly got from Mrs. Elliot before she stopped talking about the day. At first, Mrs. Elliot was more than willing to relate what happened after the moment Charlie came yelling into the farmhouse—how she grabbed for the phone and thank goodness got the operator right away; how she tore out of the house and across the yard to the tree with the broken branches; how she saw RJ lying on the ground, the kite a few feet from his head, a gaping hole in the kite ruining Charlie's carefully painted griffin. Mrs. Elliot's details often trailed away at this point. She was eager to describe the phone call, the dash across the yard, the tree, the kite. But not RJ. And now she won't mention the day at all.

Charlie strides along among the trees and he can feel

his footsteps growing harder and rougher until finally he really is on a tromp. *Tromp, tromp, tromp.* His anger is rising, and Sunny slows her pace and looks sideways at him, her brown eyes wary.

Charlie takes a deep breath. "It's all right, girl," he says. He lightens his step, but his thoughts are angry. Stupid, stupid RJ, climbing a tree and going way too high. RJ believed that he could do anything, and the rest of Lindenfield shared that opinion.

"Some hero," mutters Charlie.

Ahead Charlie sees something gleaming in the fallen leaves.

"Sunny! Stay!" he commands.

Sunny plops to the ground and sits while Charlie moves ahead. He examines the ground carefully. "Tinfoil," he says after a moment. "Okay, Sunny. Come on."

From time to time while hiking through the woods Charlie has come across a leg-hold trap, once with a rabbit, still alive, caught between the lethal jaws. That time Charlie had run for his father, shouting for him to come pry apart the trap, but Mr. Elliot had shot the rabbit almost instantly. "We're not going to be able to save him," his father had said. "And he's suffering. Looks like he's been here for a couple of days. He hasn't been able to get to food or water, and he's been attacked by something." He shakes his head. "The trappers are supposed to check their traps once every twenty-four hours."

Ever since, Charlie has been on the lookout for traps, especially when Sunny is with him. The few times he's found them, he's disabled them. What he would like to do is steal them; just lug the smaller ones home and hide them. But where? That's the part he can't figure out. Besides, if his father caught him stealing anything at all, Charlie would be in some kind of unimaginable trouble, and he's not about to risk that.

"It's okay, Sunny," Charlie says again, and obedient Sunny rises and trots toward him, sniffing the tinfoil suspiciously as she passes it.

Sunny leads the way until she comes to the stream, the one that flows into Mr. Hanna's pond. She looks back at Charlie as if to say, "Should we stop here?"

"Let's have lunch," says Charlie, dropping to the ground. He clears away some dead leaves and branches, opens his knapsack, and pulls out the sandwich, the apple, and the book. He eats the apple first, chewing thoughtfully as he watches the stream, which has a life all its own. Sunny watches the stream too. Apples are of little interest to her. But as soon as Charlie unwraps the sandwich, she abandons the stream and sits directly in front of Charlie, looking from him to the sandwich and back.

"Don't worry," says Charlie. "You know I always save you the last bite." He opens his book and reads and chews and reads and chews until one bite (of a generous size) is left. This he hands to Sunny, who accepts it so gently between her jaws that Charlie recalls that this is why RJ also used to call her Kitten Lips.

"Okay, Kitten Lips?" he says now.

Sunny is working away at the peanut butter, licking her lips. Finally, Charlie offers her his fingers so she can lick those too.

Lunch over, Charlie carefully replaces the wax paper in his knapsack. These are not his woods, but even if they were he would never litter in them. He leaves the apple core behind, though. It will be a surprise treat for a deer or a raccoon.

Now Charlie settles in with *Lassie Come-Home*. He leans against a tree trunk, and Sunny sprawls across his feet. "My feet are already hotter than blazes!" Charlie exclaims, but he can't bring himself to move her.

Charlie reads the afternoon away, reads until he realizes that the light is starting to fade and he checks his watch. "We'd better start for home," he says, getting to his feet. And boy and dog lope back to the Elliots' farm. When Charlie reaches the edge of the east field, he pauses and surveys the land. He sees no one. Everything is country serene. Which is to say that Charlie hears a pair of crows talking to each other, sees a hawk wheeling overhead, hears the wind rustling leaves and the dry stalks of tall grass, sees four deer across the field.

Charlie suspects that his father is in the barn, but has

the sense not to call out to him. Instead, he peeks through the door. There is Mr. Elliot getting ready for the big job he and his men will start on Monday. He's inventorying the cans of paint, stacking up drop cloths. The barn is quiet. Months ago Mr. Elliot stopped listening to the radio.

Charlie backs out of the barn, Sunny by his side, and crosses the yard to the house. He enters through the kitchen door. His mother has started dinner. The oven is on, and pots of vegetables from the garden are simmering on the stove. The table is set too. But where is his mother?

Charlie edges through the house. The door to his parents' bedroom is closed, so that's where his mother must be. He puts his ear to the door and hears nothing. He strays through the living room and stops. Something is different, but he isn't sure what. Then he sees that RJ's diploma now hangs over the mantelpiece, replacing nothing. Nothing was there before, and now the diploma has taken center stage.

Charlie walks back through his silent house to the kitchen to fix dinner for Sunny.

6. BONE

The next part of my tale begins with my feet. They were growing, and so was the rest of me. I knew this because Isabel and Thad kept talking about how large my feet were and how large I was getting to be in general. "Will you look at him?" said Thad one morning as he patted my back. (By this time I had been taken to the vet, and Isabel and Thad knew that I was a he, not a she.) "Those feet!" Thad exclaimed. "He really is going to be a big one." Thad seemed pleased by this.

Isabel was the woman with the long hair and the round belly, and Thad was her husband. They were nothing like Marcy and George. When Isabel brought me home from the place called the mall and I made a puddle on her floor, she just said, "No, no," and carried me outside. Sometime later, I made a puddle in the grass and then Isabel gave me a cookie and picked me up and cuddled me and told me I was a good girl. (This was before the trip to the vet.) It didn't take long for me to figure out that I should make puddles and poop when I was outside the house, and that I should never make puddles and poop when I was inside the house.

That day—the day on which I was separated from my sister and taken home with Isabel—I got a lot of new things. I got two dishes, a bed, some toys, food that came in cans, a blanket, and another name: Simone. The next day, Isabel took me to the vet and after that, my name was Simon.

"The vet says he's going to be pretty big," Isabel told Thad that evening.

Thad looked fondly at me, but he said to Isabel, "Are you sure a baby and a puppy—a big puppy—aren't going to be too much?"

Isabel shook her head and smiled. "This is the beauty of taking an extra-long maternity leave. The baby won't be born for another month and by then we'll have Simone—I mean, Simon—all trained and everything. Plus, he'll be a month older. It'll be fine."

I was sitting on the floor in my new bed. Thad reached down to pat my head, I jumped back, and he pulled his hand away, startled. "Simon's skittish," Thad remarked.

"You would be too, if someone had thrown you out a car window," replied Isabel.

Thad put his hand out again, and this time I let him give me a pat.

"Anyway, the vet said he's healthy," said Isabel. "He just needs some training."

The training began several days later. A woman with lots of pockets, and treats in every single one of them, came to the house and showed Isabel how to teach me to sit and stay and come and leave things behind and get down off of other things.

"My goodness!" said Isabel. "Those are a lot of commands."

Isabel was a patient teacher, though, and we worked together for several days. Then one evening Isabel and Thad were sitting on the couch and I was lying with my feet in Thad's lap and my head on Isabel's leg (she didn't have much lap left), when suddenly Isabel put her hands on her big belly and said, "Uh-oh."

"Honey?" said Thad. "What is it?"

"I had a pain. But it's too early for the baby."

"It's probably false labor," said Thad confidently.

A few minutes later Isabel groaned. "I don't think this is false," she said. She let out a gasp. "I think this is it. We have to go to the hospital."

This was followed by a big blur of excitement. Feet hurried back and forth and up and down the stairs. Doors opened and closed. Thad talked on the telephone. And then Isabel said, "What are we going to do about Simon?"

"Maybe your father can come over and take care of him. He likes Simon."

"All right," Isabel replied. She was puffing and holding her belly.

Thad and Isabel left the house in a hurry and for a while I was all alone in it. I needed to pee very, very badly so I sat by the door, which is how I would let Thad and Isabel know that I needed to go outside. After a long time the door suddenly opened from the other side. This was a surprise, but I took advantage of things and ran out into the night.

"Simon! Simon!" The voice belonged to Franklin Dobbs, Isabel's father. "Simon, come back here!"

I peed for a long time and went back.

Franklin Dobbs stayed in the house with me for the rest of that night and the next day and the next night and part of the following day, while Isabel was gone and Thad was mostly gone. Franklin and I were having a nap on the couch that second afternoon when I heard a noise outside. Franklin stood up and opened the door, and Thad and Isabel walked through it. Isabel was holding something in her arms and Franklin wanted to see it immediately. He talked to it very softly and said, "Oh, you are a beautiful girl." Then Isabel noticed me and said, "Simon! Hello, boy!" And Thad bent down and put his arms around my neck.

"Would you like to see the baby?" Thad asked me.

Isabel lowered herself onto the couch, patted the cushion, and said, "Come on up, Simon. Come meet Julie."

I scrambled onto the couch, put my nose in the air, and sniffed. A wonderful, delicious smell was coming from Isabel's lap. I poked my nose into the bundle of blankets and snuffled around, wagging my tail. Then I found the baby's face and gave it an exuberant lick.

"He likes her," Isabel said softly. "I think this is going to be okay."

That night, the first night the baby was with us, I sat expectantly at the door when I needed to pee. It was my regular evening peeing time, but no one noticed me. Not Franklin, who couldn't take his eyes off the baby; not Thad, who was cleaning up a number of messes; and certainly not Isabel, who was hugging the baby to her chest, something she had been doing quite a bit since she came home.

Nothing was usual about the evening. Franklin wasn't supposed to be there anymore. I knew that because Isabel kept saying, "Dad, really, you don't need to stay. Thad and Julie and I will be just fine." But Franklin kept replying, "She's my granddaughter. I can't bear to leave her yet." Then Isabel would look at her watch.

The messes Thad was cleaning up were mostly created by things having to do with the baby. For instance, there were diapers. Dirty diapers. They smelled lovely to me, and every time Thad put one in the kitchen garbage, I scratched at the cabinet door, trying to get at the pail. Once, I opened the door. I was pleased with myself, but Thad said, "What are we going to do? Simon wants the dirty diapers."

"You shouldn't be throwing them away in the kitchen," Isabel replied. She called this from the couch in the living room, where she was still sitting, the baby attached to her front. "That's disgusting. They smell too much."

"What am I supposed to do with them?" asked Thad.

"Well, where did we put the diaper pail?"

Then there was the matter of wrapping paper. Because Julie had arrived so early, Isabel and Thad's friends had not had time to give a baby shower. It turned out that this shower had something to do with gifts— and nothing to do with water—and all afternoon, people kept dropping by with presents for Julie. The presents were enclosed in paper, which Isabel and Thad peeled off and I flung about the room and tore up with my teeth. By evening, there were bits of soggy paper all over the house.

There were other messes for Thad to clean up too, and this is why, when I needed to go outside that night and I sat at the door, Thad didn't see me. He was busy cleaning. Isabel didn't see me because she was still sitting on the couch in the living room clutching Julie, and Franklin didn't see me because he was on the couch too, his eyes stuck on Julie.

I let out a whine.

I scratched at the door.

I barked.

I barked more loudly.

At last Thad said, "Oh, I think Simon needs to go out." And he opened the door. Just in time.

Later, after Franklin finally went home, Thad and Isabel climbed into their bed. They took Julie with them. I jumped up after them and was about to fling myself down in my usual spot in the very middle of the bed, when Isabel cried, "Simon! No!" and snatched up the baby. "He almost sat on Julie!" she exclaimed to Thad. "He's so big he could have smothered her."

"Honey, he's not *that* big," said Thad, although he was studying my feet again. "Still, I wonder whether it's safe for Simon to be in bed with the baby."

That night I was told to sleep on my own bed on the floor.

During the next few days, Thad found the diaper pail, and people didn't drop by quite so often, but Isabel was tired all the time. This was because Julie cried all the time. All day, all night. Thad stayed home from his job for a while, but eventually he had to go back to work, and still Julie cried and cried. Isabel held her and walked with her and sang to her. Sometimes she said, "*Please* stop crying."

I began sitting by the door more and more often. I sat there even when I didn't need to pee. It was fun to go outside, and I missed the birds and insects and grass, the sun on my fur and the wind in my face. But if I sat by the door *too* often, Isabel would say, "Simon, I don't have time for this."

One day Isabel was holding the door open for me (again) when I saw something in the bushes by the porch that made me stop in my tracks. I stopped so suddenly that Isabel nearly closed the door on my rump. I barely noticed. I stared into the bushes and barked. And barked and barked and barked.

"Simon, what on earth is it?" asked Isabel as Julie began to cry again. She peered into the bushes and saw the cat that was crouched there. "Oh, poor thing," she said. She disappeared into the house and came back without Julie. Then she closed me into the kitchen and went outside again.

By the end of the day, Isabel and Thad had added the cat to their family. Her name was Estelle, and she was fun to chase.

One night Thad came home from work and stood in the doorway and said, "Well. This is some household."

Isabel was sitting on the couch in the living room, which was an enormous mess, holding a screaming Julie. Julie could make sounds that were as loud as the screeching of an owl. I was running after Estelle, and when Estelle reached a wall and realized she couldn't go any farther, she clawed her way up the curtains and tried to balance on the rod, but the rod fell and so did Estelle and so did the curtains.

Thad took this all in and said, "I don't suppose dinner is ready yet."

Isabel looked at him in exactly the same way I had once seen Mrs. Merrion look at Mine the fox. Then she burst into tears.

"Never mind. I'll order a pizza," said Thad quickly.

"It isn't *that*!" exclaimed Isabel, and Julie cried louder and harder.

Thad picked up Julie and walked her back and forth, back and forth, through the living room. (Twice he tripped over a magazine that had fallen to the floor.) "What is it then?" he asked softly.

"Emily called today."

"Emily Steiner? From your office?"

Isabel nodded. "She reminded me that I said I would start working from home this week. And I want to. I mean, I *really* want to. I'm going crazy here. But"—she looked around at screaming Julie, the living room in its disarray, the curtains, me—"how can I do any work?" She paused. "I never even got dressed today. . . . Simon, *stop* that!"

I had discovered that Estelle was hiding beneath the fallen curtains, and I was nosing under them, my rump in the air, while Estelle hissed lustily at me.

"Simon, I said *stop* that!"

"Come on, boy. You're going to get in trouble." Thad handed Julie back to Isabel and pulled me away from the curtains. Estelle shot out of the room. I started to go after her, but Thad had a grip on my collar. "Simon," he said sternly, and I sat down. "Good boy." He turned back to Isabel. "I think it's time to start looking for a nanny," he said.

Not long after this, people started coming by, one at a time, to talk to Isabel and Thad. Each one sat in the living room (Thad had cleaned it up), and Thad and Isabel would ask the person a lot of questions about babies and cleaning and cooking and past experiences. Then the person would leave, and Isabel and Thad would have a discussion of their own. It would always end when one of them sighed deeply and said, "Well, I guess we'll have to keep looking." They were beginning to sound frustrated.

But then a woman named Zoe came by and when she left, Isabel and Thad looked at each other and grinned, and Isabel said, "She seems perfect."

"She has lots of experience," agreed Thad. "And she said she'd do light housekeeping and get dinner ready for us."

"Let's ask her to come back tomorrow so we can talk to her again," said Isabel.

Zoe returned the next day. She was a small woman, and young, who looked friendly enough, but she didn't smell right to me. I kept my distance from her. When she sat in the armchair, I crept to the far end of the room, lay down, and stared at her.

Isabel and Thad were smiling. "We wanted to talk to you a bit more," Isabel said to Zoe. "Quite honestly, you're the best person we've talked to so far. And we've talked to a *lot* of people."

"We're hoping you'll take the job," added Thad.

Zoe glanced at me (I was still staring at her) and then she looked at the carpet. "I really need the job," she said finally. "And you seem very nice, and Julie is adorable, but . . ."

"Is it the cooking?" interrupted Isabel. "You don't have to start dinner every night."

"No, it isn't that. It's, well, the dog. Cats are one thing, but dogs . . ." (I continued to stare.) "I just don't like them. And anyway, I know I'd have my hands full with Julie and the housework and everything. I wouldn't have time to walk a dog. So I'm really sorry, but I don't think this will work."

Isabel and Thad exchanged a glance. "Zoe," said Thad after a moment, "give us until tonight, okay? Don't accept any offers today. We'll call you by six o'clock."

After Zoe left, Thad and Isabel sat in the kitchen and had a long talk.

"She really is the best person we've seen," said Isabel. "Maybe we could arrange for doggie day care for Simon."

"We can't afford that. Not on top of Zoe's salary. It would hardly be worth your going back to work."

66

"I have to go back to work!" cried Isabel.

"You know what I was thinking?" said Thad a little later. "Your father has been awfully lonely since your mother died. And he loves Simon. Maybe . . ."

"Simon *is* good company," agreed Isabel. "And it's true that Dad loves him. But do you think he can handle a dog? He's starting to slow down. And he didn't get a very good report from his doctor last week."

"I think Simon is exactly what your father needs," said Thad heartily. "Your dad'll get out of the house, start taking walks again. It'll be perfect."

"I suppose."

Two days later, Isabel and Thad packed up my toys and my bed and my food and drove me to Franklin's apartment. They took me inside and said, "Good-bye, Simon," and, "We love you, Simon," and even though Franklin tried to coax me onto the couch with him, I sat at his door for a very long time, waiting for it to open from the other side.

7. HENRY

Henry's first day at school without Matthew passed uneventfully. At recess he sat outside on a bench next to the back door of Claremont Elementary. He thought about how this year he was one of the oldest students in his school, and next year, when he entered middle school, he would be one of the youngest. He studied his Carlos Beltrán baseball card. Then he made a drawing of Owen pitching to Antony in the daily recess softball game.

After a while, Henry lost interest in drawing and baseball and Owen and Antony, and he listened to the teachers on playground duty discuss the stock market.

"Luckily, most of our investments are in municipal bonds," said one. "They're much safer."

Municipal bonds, thought Henry. He would have to find out what they were.

The other teacher replied, "We decided to get rid of all our bank holdings. They seem too risky right now."

"Bank holdings. Hmm." Henry pulled out a pad of paper and made some notes.

The bell rang then and Henry's classmates streamed past him and into the corridor. Henry joined the end of the line. If only he knew that a dog named Buddy would be waiting for him when he got home.

At dinner that night, Henry expected his parents to mention the Christmas list. Neither one did. They didn't mention it the next day or the day after that. What was wrong? Had they not noticed that he had resurrected his two-year-old list? That was how badly he still wanted a dog and a doghouse and everything for a dog. Maybe the list was too sloppy, and his tidy librarian parents hadn't liked the look of all the cross-outs.

Or maybe, thought Henry as he sat on the bench on the playground again one afternoon, his parents hadn't even read the list yet. Maybe it had gotten lost in the giant stack of mail on the counter. Henry ran home from school that day—pelted all the way down Nassau Street, around the corner, and along Tinker Lane to his house. He let himself inside and made a beeline for the pile of papers in the kitchen. He shuffled through the stack, didn't see the list, and shuffled through the papers once more, just to make sure. No list. Where was it? Henry was wondering whether it would be all right to search his parents' desk when he glanced across the kitchen and saw that the list had been smoothed out and posted on the refrigerator. It was right there in plain sight where his parents could look at it day after day. He noticed that someone, probably his mother, had put a large red exclamation point on the top of the page. This, Henry supposed, meant that his parents were amused by the list. They hadn't taken it seriously. They also hadn't mentioned the list, Christmas, and certainly not the request for a dog.

Henry thought back to the last time he had asked his parents for a dog. The conversation, which had taken place just two months earlier, had not gone well. It had started when Henry said, "Remember when we went to the animal shelter?"

His father replied, "I do. We adopted Amelia Earhart. That was fun."

"Maybe it's time for another fun visit," Henry had said.

His father, who had been reading on the couch, put his book down, removed his glasses, and looked squarely at Henry.

"Could we go just to look at the animals?" Henry had asked.

"Just to look?" his father repeated.

"At the dogs," said Henry.

"But just to look."

"Well, at first. But then maybe we could come home, talk about what we looked at, and go back again."

Henry's father was quiet, so finally Henry had said, "Dad, please can't I have a dog? *Please?*"

Henry's mother had joined them then. She sat on the arm of the couch and said, "A dog, Henry? Haven't we already had this discussion? Several times?"

"Yes, but I'm eleven now."

Henry's mother had let out a long sigh. "I know what will happen if we get a dog," she said. "You'll love it and play with it, but your father and I will be the ones who wind up walking it and feeding it and training it and cleaning up its messes. Do you know how much work a dog involves?"

Henry had shrugged. He hadn't given much thought to those things. He just wanted a dog.

Now he thought about that conversation and realized his parents had been trying to tell him something. They had been trying to say that they *still* hadn't thought he was responsible enough to care for a dog. Huh. Well, maybe that really had been true when Henry was younger. But now he was almost ready for middle school. He was much more mature and responsible. He just needed to prove that to his parents.

"Aha!" said Henry aloud. "That's the key."

The next morning when Henry's mother knocked on his bedroom door and called, "Henry! Time to get going!" Henry opened the door with a flourish and grinned.

He was fully dressed.

"Don't forget to make your b—"

Henry indicated his bed. It was neatly made.

After breakfast, Henry lugged the overflowing recycling cans from the garage down to the bottom of the driveway.

"Henry," said his father when Henry reappeared in the kitchen, "remember, today is recycling day. You—"

Henry led his father to the front door and pointed to the street.

His father looked at him in surprise. "You remembered!" he said. "And you did the job perfectly."

"Thank you," Henry replied modestly.

When school ended that day, Henry left his classroom and walked past the gym and the office to the library where his mother was sitting at her desk working at the computer.

"Hello," said Henry.

"Well, this is a surprise," his mother replied.

"I thought I'd walk home with you today."

Henry and his mother walked through Claremont, and Henry said he had heard there was a big school board meeting coming up. "I certainly hope the budget passes," he added.

His mother looked curiously at him, but Henry walked along as if he always thought about school boards and budgets.

The moment they got home, Henry sat down at the kitchen table and started his assignments. When he was finished, he carried his books upstairs and set them in a neat pile on his dresser. He looked around his room and decided it was a bit messy, so he spent some time tidying it. He picked up all the things that were lying on the floor and put them where they belonged. Then he crawled under his bed to see what might be there. He found a lot of clothes, two CDs without their cases, and some pencils he thought he'd lost. He was about to put the under-the-bed clothes away when he realized they had been there for so many months that they no longer fit him, so he laid them on his chair. He thought that some of the shirts hanging in his closet were now too tight, and that at least one pair of shoes had also become too tight. He gathered up the too-small articles of clothing and stacked them neatly in a shopping bag. After that, he opened his wallet, took out all of his money, and placed it in an envelope. He carried the shopping bag and the envelope downstairs.

"What's this?" asked his mother.

"Well," said Henry, "I cleaned out my closet and these are the things that don't fit me anymore. I thought we should give them to the Family Center. I know how you hate sorting through my clothes, and I wanted to save you the trouble. While I was at it, I decided to make a donation to the animal shelter, so here's all my money." He held out the envelope.

Henry's mother looked at him with her mouth open.

Then she pulled Henry to her and gave him a hug. "I am so proud of you," she said.

At dinner that night Henry waited until everyone had been served before he said, "I've been thinking about our investments lately. Maybe we should give up our bank holdings and put everything into municipal bonds."

"What?" said his father.

"It just makes sense. Munies are very reliable."

"Munies . . ." murmured his mother.

"That's short for municipal bonds. It's sort of their nickname. Anyway," said Henry, "I'm just watching out for our," he paused, "for our assets. And our future."

Henry's mother looked across the table at his father. "Chas," she said, "do you know what Henry did this afternoon? He cleaned up his room—unasked—sorted through his clothes, bagged up the ones that don't fit him anymore, and also made a donation to the animal shelter."

"I haven't actually *made* the donation. Not yet," said Henry. "The envelope is still here. Mom said we'll take it to the shelter on Monday."

"This is all very impressive," said Henry's father, "but is there anything you'd like to tell us?"

Henry looked at his father in surprise. "What do you mean?"

"Are we going to find a message from one of your teachers when we check our e-mail tonight?"

"No!" exclaimed Henry. "You think I did something *wrong*? Is that it? You think I'm covering something up?"

"I'm sorry. It's just that I can't help but remember how clean the house was after you and Matthew erased the library files from our computer."

"We didn't do that on purpose!"

"I know you didn't. The point is that before you confessed to your mother and me—and, by the way, we were very proud of you for telling the truth—you tried to soften the blow by vacuuming the bedrooms."

"And washing the kitchen floor," added Henry.

"Yes."

Henry put his fork down. The conversation was not going as he had hoped.

"So, is there anything—anything at all," said his father, "that you'd like to share with us now?"

Henry shook his head. "No. I was just trying to show you something. Actually, I was trying to prove something to you."

"What was that?" asked his mother gently.

"I was trying to prove that I'm responsible enough to be a dog owner. I'll be in *middle* school next year. I can do things without being told. And I don't mean," he said hastily, realizing that he had been on his good behavior for scarcely twelve hours, "that I'm going to be a responsible person for just a day or two. I mean that's who I am now—a mature and responsible son who will take very good care of a dog. All by myself."

By this time, nobody at the table was eating. Henry's hands were in his lap and his dinner was growing cold. His father was sitting in front of a nearly full plate of food. And his mother had pushed her plate away and folded her arms on the edge of the table.

Henry's father drew in a deep breath. He opened his mouth to speak, closed his mouth, and then opened it again. At last he said, "I'm very, very sorry, but we are not going to get a dog."

Henry turned to his mother. She shook her head.

"But why?" cried Henry. *"Why?"*

"For one thing," said his father, "the dog would be home alone for most of the day while we're at work and you're at school. That's not fair."

"Amelia Earhart is alone all day," Henry pointed out.

"Cats are different from dogs," said his mother. "They don't need to go outside to go to the bathroom. And they don't mind being alone. Dogs want company."

"Also," his father continued, "dogs are much more work than you imagine. You have to housebreak them, and that's a big job. And they need lots of exercise. Our yard isn't fenced in, so that means that if we had a dog it would need to be taken on walks every day."

"And, of course, you need to feed a dog and clean up after it," added his mother.

"Furthermore," said his father, "dogs are expensive."

Henry was tempted to say, *More expensive than cats?* but instead he said nothing at all.

"Besides, you have Amelia Earhart, Carlos Beltran, and Hamlet," said his mother.

Henry felt anger rising up from somewhere deep inside. He thought of telling his parents that they were thoughtless and cruel, but he had a feeling that such behavior might appear immature, and he was not yet ready to give up on his plan.

8. CHARLIE

Charlie can't remember a summer vacation as quiet as the one that is now unfolding. The mornings are particularly quiet. His father rises early, eats in a hurry, and goes to the barn to gather the supplies he and his men will need that day. Charlie gets up next. He feeds Sunny, then himself. Pop-Tarts make a good breakfast if anyone has remembered to buy them. If it's one of the days Charlie will be working at Mr. Hanna's, he leaves the house at nine-thirty. If it isn't a Mr. Hanna day, Charlie sometimes goes to work with his father and sometimes just wanders around the farm. His mother hasn't been getting up before ten. By the time school has been out for four days, she's staying in bed until at least eleven. These mornings are so different from the mornings of a year ago that Charlie can barely stand to remember the old summer days. When he does—when he recalls Sunny leaping to her feet at the sight of RJ, and his mother laughing as she fixes eggs and bacon, and the radio with Cousin Brucie and Ron Lundy playing the sizzling summer hits (*if* Charlie's mother will allow the

78

rock and roll station)—those summer days seem to belong to another family somewhere else, another family that's now as lost as RJ.

"I wish I were back in school," Charlie tells Sunny one morning. When school was in session, Charlie's mind was occupied with homework and lessons and friends. Now his mind sometimes seems as empty as his days, and what tiptoes into all that emptiness in his mind? RJ. A morning at Mr. Hanna's is good and a day spent on the job with his father is good, but a day in which the emptiness creeps in is unbearable.

On Wednesday morning Charlie discovers that the Pop-Tarts box is empty, so he eats a bowl of cereal, sitting alone at the kitchen table. His father has already driven down their lane in the pickup. Charlie can hear birds calling and the wind soughing in the firs and in the distance a tractor, but that's it. The quiet is unnerving. He considers turning on the radio to see if he can find the top ten, but his mother is asleep and Charlie doesn't think he can bear to listen to Cousin Brucie alone. At the stroke of nine-thirty he hightails it to Mr. Hanna's.

"I hope you got your muscles ready today, boy," is how Mr. Hanna greets him. He's standing on his stoop hefting a hatchet. "It's never too early to lay in firewood."

Charlie grins. He likes splitting logs. He's not sure his mother would allow him to do such work, but she was still asleep when Charlie left the house, so Charlie doesn't care what she would allow. He spends the first part of the morning splitting dozens of logs while Sunny dozes in the shade. Later he paints Mr. Hanna's two Adirondack chairs using a bucket of Forest Shade he brought over on Monday. When Charlie is done, Mr. Hanna fixes lunch—tomato sandwiches for himself and Charlie, and a bowl of water for Sunny who isn't supposed to eat lunch since the vet estimates that she's five pounds overweight.

After lunch Charlie is disappointed when Mr. Hanna hands him his pay. He's grateful for the money—it's more than he expected; that isn't the problem—but he doesn't want to go home yet; had, in fact, hoped to work all afternoon. Maybe he could take Sunny on a walk through the woods. He doesn't have a book with him, though, and Sunny is wilting in the heat like his mother's pansies, so finally he leaves the woods behind and enters the expectant rooms of his house through the back door.

The house sounds empty.

"Mom?" Charlie calls.

He hears Sunny's toenails clicking as she makes her way into the bathroom to cool herself on the tile floor.

"Mom?" he calls again.

There is no answer. After a while Charlie finds his mother sitting in a rocking chair on the front porch. She's crying. Just sitting and crying. Charlie backs away.

The next day is not a Mr. Hanna day, and Mr. Elliot

drives off before Charlie is up. Mrs. Elliot doesn't leave her room. Not the entire long day. Charlie listens at the bedroom door and can hear her crying. He wishes he knew where his father was working so he could phone him.

Charlie brings his mother water. He makes her tea. He offers to read to her. But she won't get out of bed and she won't stop crying.

Charlie and Sunny wait on the front porch for Mr. Elliot to return. When at last he does, when the shadows are lengthening and the air is cooling and Charlie thinks that this endless day may have an end to it after all, Mr. Elliot disappears inside to see to Charlie's mother, and Charlie sits and waits and thinks about RJ.

Charlie sits for so long that his stomach begins to rumble and he decides to make dinner. But when he steps into the living room he finds his father speaking nervously into the phone, twisting the cord around his fingers.

"Dad?" Charlie says in a loud whisper.

His father puts his hand over the mouthpiece. "Not now, Charlie," he says. "I have to . . . to make some calls." He shifts his body so that he's facing away from Charlie.

Two days later, Charlie's aunt Susan arrives. She steers her aged Studebaker along the Elliots' drive and climbs out of it with a bag of groceries, three books for Charlie, and warm bosomy hugs for everyone including Sunny.

Charlie has met his aunt, his father's older sister, only a

handful of times, but he's grateful for her appearance now. Mr. Elliot hasn't left the house since the night he phoned Susan, and to Charlie his parents seem to be spirits drifting through the rooms, his mother weeping, his father cajoling and occasionally losing his temper. Mrs. Elliot, Charlie knows, is going to go back to Susan's home and rest there for a while. Charlie suspects it will be a long while. Like maybe until the end of the summer.

Aunt Susan stays for lunch, which she makes (and which Mrs. Elliot doesn't eat), but as soon as it's over she says, "I guess we'd better hit the road."

Charlie glances at his mother, who is sitting at the table right next to Aunt Susan and appears not to have heard her.

Mr. Elliot has tears in his eyes, and Charlie cannot bear to see him cry again, so he runs up the stairs to his room to watch the leave-taking from a distance. His room is roasting, but he closes his windows so he won't have to hear any of the words in the yard below. He watches his father take his mother by the elbow and lead her toward Susan's car, watches him stow her suitcase in the backseat, watches him hug his sister and kiss his wife and wave to the car as it creeps down the lane. Mr. Elliot looks up at Charlie's window then, but Charlie ducks away. He can't ignore the knock on his door a minute later, though.

"We're on our own now," says Mr. Elliot as he sits on the edge of Charlie's bed.

"For how long?" Charlie wants to know.

Mr. Elliot shakes his head slowly. "Until things are better," he says at last.

The next day is Sunday and when Charlie and his father go to church, Charlie is reminded of how fast news travels in Lindenfield. It seems that everyone already knows that Mrs. Elliot has gone away for a while.

RJ is lost, and Mrs. Elliot has gone away. For a while.

For the whole summer, guesses Charlie.

He averts his eyes when people press their hands on his father's arm or pat his back. "We'll bring a casserole by tonight," they say. Or a pot roast or corn muffins or a three-bean salad. And they do. The neighbors start arriving not long after church (during which they prayed for "our dear Doreen Elliot who has gone away for a while"). By suppertime the neighbors have left and the kitchen is so full of food that Charlie and his father don't quite know where to put it all.

"I guess we won't have to test our cooking skills," says Mr. Elliot in a very bright tone of voice. "At least not right away. What would you like for dinner tonight, Charlie?"

"I don't care."

"Well," his father continues in the same perky voice, "we have everything but fried worms here." Charlie still does not smile, so his father sighs and says, "All right. Roast chicken and potato salad."

Charlie feeds Sunny while his father serves up their

supper. When they are seated at the kitchen table, just the two of them, the other two chairs now empty, Mr. Elliot says, "We'll have to make some changes around here for the summer. Your mother's egg business has to be seen to. And she started the vegetable garden before ..." He pauses. "Well, she started it, and we need to keep up with it. That'll be your job, Charlie. And we'll both take care of the chickens."

Charlie nods. He doesn't mind either of these things, although he doesn't think the garden will flourish under his care the way it does when his mother tends it.

"I'm afraid you're going to be alone a lot this summer," Mr. Elliot continues.

"Not really," says Charlie. "I'll be at Mr. Hanna's, or I can work with you, and I always have Sunny."

"Still, it doesn't sound like much of a summer."

Charlie shrugs. It wasn't much of a summer *before* his mother went away.

Charlie and his father eat in silence until Mr. Elliot says, "Mr. Trego spoke to me in church this morning."

Mr. Trego is the music teacher at Jackson Elementary.

"Oh, yeah?" says Charlie.

"He wanted to know if you'd take RJ's place in the Fourth of July parade on Tuesday."

"Take his place? How can I do that?" RJ played the trumpet in the school band, which will be marching in

84

the parade along with the Girl Scouts, the Boy Scouts, the firemen, the Little League team, and the High Notes, a singing group Mrs. Elliot used to belong to. "I don't play the trumpet," says Charlie. "I don't play any instrument."

"Mr. Trego just wanted you to march in RJ's spot in the formation—as a tribute to your brother."

Charlie feels heavy, as if a great weight is pushing down on him. He cannot take his brother's place again, can't accept one more honor for him or speak for him or play his role. Even as a tribute to him.

"Dad," he says finally, "I'd be embarrassed walking along without an instrument."

His father lowers his eyes. "It's your decision," he replies. "Call Mr. Trego tomorrow and tell him."

Charlie knows better than to ask his father to make the call. "Can I call him tonight?" he says instead. "To get it over with?"

His father shakes his head. "It's Sunday."

But then the phone rings and Charlie rushes to answer it. If it's Mr. Trego calling *him*, he would have a perfect right to give him the news now.

The caller is Aunt Susan, however. "Just checking in," she says, "to see how you boys are doing."

Charlie almost smiles at this, at his father's being called a boy. "We're fine," he tells her. "How's Mom?"

There is a slight pause, like a breath, before his aunt says, "I'll put her on the phone."

"No!" yelps Charlie. "I mean, wait. Let me get Dad." He drops the receiver with a clunk and calls, "Dad! It's Aunt Susan. Mom wants to talk to you. I'm going to take Sunny on a walk."

In a flash he's out the door.

On the Fourth of July all of Lindenfield is dressed for the holiday. Flags fly from doorways and the handlebars of bicycles. Red, white, and blue swags swathe the lampposts in town. Mr. Hanson sells red-and-blue Italian ices from his cart. Charlie finds a red-white-and-blue-striped T-shirt to wear to the parade, and he puts a red-and-white bandanna around Sunny's neck, even though Sunny won't be going into town. She can wear it later, just to look festive.

The day before, Charlie called Mr. Trego, who was understanding when Charlie said he would prefer not to march with the band. "It was just a thought," said Mr. Trego.

"We're still going to come to the parade," Charlie informed him, relieved.

Now, on Tuesday, as Charlie and his father approach Dean Avenue in their truck and Charlie catches sight of all that red, white, and blue, and hears the bleat of a trombone in the distance, and somewhere, even farther away, the *pop-pop-pop* of firecrackers, he feels a little prickle of excitement. Maybe he and his dad can go to the fireworks show at the high school stadium that night. Charlie tries to decide when might be the best time to ask his father about that.

Mr. Elliot parks the pickup behind the Everything Else Store, and he and Charlie find spots on the sidewalk in front of Jackson Elementary.

"Dad," says Charlie suddenly, guilt-ridden, "we should have asked Mr. Hanna to come with us," and just as suddenly he catches sight of Mr. Hanna down the block.

Mr. Elliot waves to him and Mr. Hanna makes his way through the crowd to stand with Charlie and his father. Charlie feels that prickle of excitement again. It's a glorious day for a Fourth of July parade. The sky is as blue as an indigo bunting and the air is clear and warm and everywhere people are shouting and calling to one another. Children are clutching tiny flags as their Italian ices drip down their chins and wrists. The people who greet Mr. Elliot do so cautiously, but Charlie ignores them, craning his head to the right for the first glimpse of the parade. Soon he can feel the beat of a bass drum in his stomach, and then there are the High Notes, leading off the parade. The Girl Scouts go by, followed by the Boy Scouts, and then Charlie sees two of RJ's classmates in majorette uniforms carrying a banner that reads JACKSON ELEMENTARY. Behind them is the band and as it passes by, Charlie realizes that the space that would have been occupied by the trumpet player, RJ's space, has been left open.

Charlie glances at his father and sees tears slipping down his cheeks as he cries silently, and the day is ruined. He knows now that his father came into town only to see the band, and that going to the fireworks is out of the question.

When the parade is over, Charlie and his father drive back to the farm. Mr. Elliot heads directly for the barn to get ready for the next day's job, and now it is a summer day like any other. Charlie whistles for Sunny, forgetting about her dashing bandanna, and they lope through the field toward the woods. Sunny startles at the bang of a firecracker, and Charlie watches the tail of a kite disappear above a stand of trees.

His family is dissolving.

9. BONE

My days with Franklin Dobbs were very different from my days with Isabel and Thad and Julie and Estelle. Mainly this was because Franklin and I were the only ones at home, so Franklin's apartment was quiet, even with the TV playing all the time.

I liked Franklin and the couch he sat on most of the day, but I missed a lot of things. I missed running through the house chasing after Estelle. I missed playing with Thad, who would throw balls for me in the yard. I missed the lady with the treats in her pockets. And I missed things from before. I missed romping in the woods with Squirrel. I missed the world of the Merrions' yard, even if Squirrel and I sometimes found danger there.

Franklin Dobbs was nice to me, but our days were like the shed at dawn, before the world had wakened.

Sometimes Isabel came by to check on her father, and then things were more interesting. She would bring Julie with her and I would watch Julie who was growing bigger and who could creep around by herself now, on all fours like me.

"Are you getting out and walking?" Isabel asked her father one morning.

"Well . . ." he replied. "Well, it's a little easier to drive."

"I mean, are you walking with Simon?" said Isabel. "You could walk around the block with him."

"My knees aren't what they used to be," Franklin answered.

"It would be good for both of you," Isabel insisted.

Franklin spread his hands. "My doctor says I should be using a cane now."

"Oh, I see," said Isabel, looking troubled. "A cane and a dog. I guess that would be difficult to manage." She glanced out the window. "So where does he, you know, do his business?"

"I just let him out the back door. Mr. Bruce has been very nice about that. As long as I clean up the poop every now and then," he added. "Which actually I haven't done yet."

Isabel rose and looked into the tiny yard behind the building owned by Mr. Bruce. The yard was enclosed by brick walls. "That's not a very big space," she remarked. "There isn't room for him to run around. There's not even much for him to sniff."

"Simon is good company," said Franklin cautiously. "Sleeps right here on the couch with me all day."

It was true. I did sleep a lot at Franklin's. When I was

90

asleep I didn't notice that we weren't taking walks or playing with balls.

One thing Franklin could still do was drive, and usually when he got into his car he let me get in with him. He made me sit behind him, but that was okay. I looked out the windows and watched the world passing by. Franklin drove me to the grocery store and into town and sometimes around the countryside and once to a fascinating place called the dump, which had excellent smells.

One morning when I had been living with Franklin for several seasons, he said he needed to go to the grocery store to buy bananas and Milk-Bones. I was gazing out the window of the car, looking longingly at a chipmunk searching for food by the side of the road, when I heard a terrific crash and I was thrown across the backseat. Franklin cried out and the car skidded noisily and came to a stop when it ran over a mailbox. After the crash I didn't hear anything for a few moments. Finally, I peered into the front seat. Franklin was slumped over the steering wheel and he wasn't moving, but when I scrambled forward and licked his ear he made a little moaning sound.

From outside the car I could hear shouts and someone opened Franklin's door and said, "Are you okay, sir?"

Someone else said, "He pulled out without even looking. We could all have been killed."

"But we weren't," said the first person, a man. "We're

fine, and I think this guy is going to be okay. It looks like his dog is all right too."

After that, a lot of things happened, and they happened fast, so I don't remember them very well. Someone pulled a telephone out of her pocket and made a call. Soon a white truck came wailing down the street and the man who had opened Franklin's door said, "Good. Here's the ambulance."

Franklin woke up and the woman asked him if she could call anyone, and not long after the ambulance took Franklin away, Thad arrived in his car and dropped me off at the house with Julie and Estelle and the woman who didn't like dogs.

I stayed there for a few days, but soon Isabel returned me to Franklin's apartment. I found him lying on the couch with a bandage on his head and another on his arm and another on his hand.

"I really don't see how you're going to care for Simon, Dad," said Isabel. "You can barely walk, and you aren't allowed to drive anymore."

"But I miss him," said Franklin, and he had a look on his face that was very sad. "I miss Simon when he isn't here. It's lonely without him." He reached out to give me a pat.

Isabel wore the same sad look on her face when she said, "You know, we've been investigating assisted-living situations for you, Dad. Thad and I feel that you should live in a place where you can get some help every day. We think living alone is too much for you."

"Didn't you arrange for Meals on Wheels?" asked Franklin.

"Yes, but that only solves one problem."

Franklin sighed heavily. When Isabel was gone, he said to me, "My daughter. She means well, but she doesn't understand. I don't want to leave my home."

There were many problems in those days, but a new one was that sometimes Franklin didn't remember to let me out into the yard anymore. I sat at the door and whined and even barked, and Franklin would say, "Simon, be quiet, boy. You're bothering the neighbors."

I made a few messes by the door. I didn't know what else to do.

Isabel and Thad and the nice man who came by with meals, and who smelled of turkey and cheese and eggs and bread, noticed the messes.

"Dad?" said Isabel one evening. "Are you remembering to let Simon outside?"

"He goes out," Franklin replied. He was staring at a teacup.

"I mean regularly."

Franklin didn't answer.

It was not too long after this that Isabel and Thad came by together one afternoon and sat down in Franklin's living room with no smiles on their faces. "We need to have a serious discussion, Dad," said Isabel.

Franklin grunted.

"We've found a very nice place for you to move to," said Thad. "You'll have your own suite of rooms and you can eat in the dining room."

"No more cooking," put in Isabel. "And all there in the same complex are a small bank and a post office—"

"An activities room," added Thad, "and a barber shop and a coffee shop and a gift shop—"

"What do I want with a gift shop?" asked Franklin.

"A swimming pool and an auditorium," Isabel continued. "And you can go on field trips—"

"Like to the zoo and the fire station?" said Franklin crabbily.

"Dad, we were lucky to get a spot for you. Usually these places have very long waiting lists. But you'll be able to move in two weeks."

"Where is this magical place?" asked Franklin.

"Right in Skillman. You'll only be five miles away. Isabel and Julie and I can visit you all the time," Thad replied.

Franklin grunted again.

"The only problem," said Isabel, and her voice became soft, like Matthias's when he used to hold me and stroke me, "is that you can't take Simon with you. No pets allowed."

Franklin looked away but I saw that his eyes were wet.

The next days were very busy. Isabel and Thad came by to pack up Franklin's clothes and to help him decide which pieces of furniture he would bring with him to his new home. Somebody else came by to take away the things he said he didn't need.

"I'll sell them for a good price," the man told Isabel.

Franklin's eyes were wet again.

When Isabel and the man left, Franklin's apartment was much emptier. Franklin eased himself down onto his old couch. He patted the cushions. "This couch stays with me," he said. "It goes wherever I go." Then he looked at me and I saw that tears were sliding down his cheeks. "No pets allowed," said Franklin, and he shook his head. "I never heard of such a rule."

I jumped up onto the couch, and Franklin wrapped his arms around me.

In the days that were left before he moved, Franklin patted me and hugged me a lot. He whispered to me and told me I was a good boy and a good friend. Some nights he was too tired to climb into his bed, so we slept together on the couch by the watery light of the TV, my chin resting on Franklin's chest.

Franklin and I slept like that on his very last night in the apartment. When Franklin woke up in the deepest part of the night to go to the bathroom, I stood at the front door and whined, so Franklin let me outside into the little yard. I sniffed and peed and walked around and sniffed and peed and walked around, and then I saw a cat sitting on top of one of the brick walls. I stood below her and barked energetically until Mr. Bruce raised his window with a crash and shouted at me and tried to spray me with a squirt gun. "What are you doing out here at this hour, anyway?" he said in a voice that was just as loud as my barking. "You're a nuisance and a pest—"

At that moment Franklin let me back inside and we spent the rest of the night asleep on the couch.

The next morning Isabel and Thad arrived early, and then a truck pulled up outside the apartment building.

"The movers are here, Dad," said Isabel.

Franklin would not answer her. He hugged me tightly.

Isabel let the movers in. Later, while they were loading things into the van, Franklin said, "What are you going to do about Simon?"

"We haven't quite figured that out," Isabel replied, "but you know we'll do something. Maybe he can even come visit you once you're settled."

"I thought pets weren't allowed."

"Maybe visiting pets are."

Franklin scowled.

For the next little while, the movers carried things out of the apartment one after another until finally the rooms were bare like the branches of the trees outside the window. Franklin and Isabel and Thad and I had nothing to sit on, so Isabel said, "Dad, come on, let's get in the car. I'm going to drive you to your new home, and Thad's going to follow us a little later."

Franklin turned from Isabel to me. "Well, Simon," he said. "Well, boy." He tried to bend down, but he couldn't lean over very far, so I stood and rested my front paws on his knees and he ruffled the fur on my head. He opened his mouth and I thought he was going to say something more, but instead he straightened up and followed Isabel out of the apartment.

Thad watched them from the window. Then he looked all around the empty apartment and finally he looked at me. He produced a telephone from his pocket, put his finger on a button, and then put the phone back in his pocket.

"Simon, stay, boy," he said. He left the apartment. When he returned, Mr. Bruce was with him. Mr. Bruce's face was not happy.

"It won't be for very long," Thad was saying. "Just until we can figure out what to do with him. A few days at most."

"Why can't you take him?" asked Mr. Bruce.

Thad shook his head. "It's our babysitter. She doesn't like dogs. She almost quit when Simon stayed with us after the accident. And we can't afford to lose her."

Mr. Bruce scratched his head. "I don't know. Isn't the dog going to be lonely here by himself? And what am I supposed to feed him?"

"There's leftover chow in the kitchen," said Thad, "and I'll run out and get him a bed so he doesn't have to sleep on the bare floor." When Mr. Bruce didn't say anything, Thad added hurriedly, "All you'll have to do is fill his food dish and let him out in the yard a few times a day. I hate to ask this, but our hands are tied."

"All *right*," said Mr. Bruce at last, sounding as if it really was not all right. "But just for a few days. Where's his collar?"

Thad shrugged. "I don't know. I guess he can do without one for now." He left then and that was when my days became not only quiet but lonely. I lay on the bed that Thad bought. I stood on my hind legs and looked out the window. I ate my chow when Mr. Bruce came by, and I peed and pooped in the yard.

That was it.

Mr. Bruce didn't speak to me. He entered the apartment with a frown on his face, gave me my food, let me outside, let me back inside, and then left me alone again. Finally, one day he did say something to me. He said, "Haven't heard a blasted word about what's going to happen to you."

He walked out of the apartment and left the door open behind him. I stood still for a bit, and then peered into the hallway. In one direction was the door to the yard. I tiptoed in the other direction until I came to the front door of the building. I found this one open too. Wide open. Beyond it were cars and the street and more buildings, all the things I had seen from Franklin's windows.

I set off down the street and didn't look back.

10. CHARLIE

On July fifth, Charlie makes a decision. He has two months of summer vacation left, and he doesn't want to go back to school in September feeling as though the entire vacation slipped by him. Maybe RJ has been lost, and maybe Charlie's mother is away, and maybe his father is largely absent, but Charlie can still have a vacation. He'll just have to be in charge of it. So he decides to make a list of things he would like to do this summer. He sits on the front porch that afternoon with a pad of paper and a pencil and a plate of brownies from one of the church ladies.

"We can make this a good summer," Charlie tells Sunny, feeling slightly less confident than he sounds. "It's just that it's up to us. Well, really it's up to me." He pauses. "I know what *you* want to do, girl. You want to go on plenty of walks in the woods and come with me to Mr. Hanna's. You'd like to ride in the pickup too, but I can't help you there."

Charlie gazes thoughtfully across the yard to the fir trees. He sighs. Then he turns back to his list. "First thing," he says, "is swimming. I want to go swimming in the river with Danny. You could come along for that, Sunny."

Charlie calls his list Things To Do This Summer. He thinks for a moment before adding the word *Fun* at the beginning of the title.

Then he writes 1. Go swimming with Danny and realizes how long it's been since he and his friend Danny went off on one of their adventures together. It's possible that this hasn't happened since RJ died.

Charlie turns back to the list.

2. Check ten books out of library every week

3. Work in vegetable garden

As he writes the third item, Charlie realizes something else: He wants to make a success of the garden. He wants to do it for his mother and for his father, but also for himself, just to prove that he can. He knows little about gardening, but he could probably find some books about it when he goes to the library.

4. Catch fireflies (let them loose later)

5. Make Dad go on picnic in woods

6. Build something (what?)

7. Go to county fair

8. Camp outside in yard with Danny

Charlie thinks this is a fine start for his summer plans, although he'll need cooperation from an adult in order to do several of the things on the list, and isn't sure he'll get it from his father. "If I don't," he says aloud to Sunny, "then I'll talk to Mr. Hanna. I'll bet he'd like to go to the fair. He could help me build something too. And when he drives into town, I could ride along with him and go to the library."

So Charlie begins his summer, this summer on his own. The first thing he does is call Danny. "Want to go swimming tomorrow afternoon?" he asks.

"What? Really?"

"Yeah."

"In the river where we used to go—"

Charlie senses that Danny was going to add "with RJ," so he steps on Danny's words, saying, "We could bring Sunny along. And sandwiches! You should see how much food is in our kitchen."

"Cool," says Danny. Then, "Who's going to drive you to the swimming spot?"

"Mr. Hanna," Charlie replies with certainty (although he hasn't asked him about this). "Or I'll walk. I don't mind that it's far."

"Cool," says Danny again. "I'll see you there tomorrow."

"Two o'clock," says Charlie. "I'll be done with my job by then."

Mr. Hanna happily drives Charlie and Sunny to the swimming spot the next afternoon and stays to watch them splash around with Danny. The day after that, he drives Charlie into town. While Mr. Hanna shops in the hardware store, Charlie prowls the stacks in the library. He chooses eight books in the fiction section of the children's room, and then approaches the librarian at her desk.

"Hello, Charlie," she says, and Charlie is pleased that she neither asks how his mother is nor says a word about RJ.

"Hi," Charlie replies.

"Ready to check out?"

"Not yet. I only have eight books here. I can take out two more, and I need to learn about gardening. Do you have any books on vegetable gardens?"

The librarian helps Charlie find two books and that night Charlie begins to pore through them. Mr. Elliot sits next to him on the couch while Sunny curls up next to Charlie's leg, making herself quite small.

"Dad, it looks like we can plant peas again in the fall," says Charlie, "when the weather gets cool. Did Mom ever do that?"

Mr. Elliot frowns. "Maybe," he says. "I'm not sure. You can ask her when she calls tonight."

And Charlie does. It's the first time he's spoken to her since she drove off with Aunt Susan.

"Plant peas again?" she repeats when Charlie tells her about his trip to the library. She sounds weary.

"Yes," says Charlie. "I was just wondering, because the book says peas like cool weather, and they have a short growing season."

"You're right about that. And yes, sometimes I do put peas in again. You just have to clear out the old vines first. Charlie, I'm . . . I'm glad you've taken over the garden."

"Thank you," Charlie replies politely, as if he's talking to his principal or to some relative he's never met before.

By the beginning of August, Charlie has ticked several more things off of his list—catching fireflies, camping with Danny, and building a footstool with Mr. Hanna. Charlie secretly decides to give the stool to his mother when she comes home. Amazingly, Charlie and his father have plans to go to the county fair in two weeks. Most important, in Charlie's eyes, is that the vegetable garden is doing nearly as well as it did when Mrs. Elliot was in charge of it.

"Mom!" says Charlie excitedly when his mother phones one night. "I picked so many cucumbers today that Dad and I had to give most of them away. I took some to Mr. Hanna, and Dad's going to give some to the guys at work. And we have peppers and lots of tomatoes and you should see how much squash we're going to have this fall."

"Honey, that's wonderful," exclaims Mrs. Elliot, and Charlie thinks she sounds stronger and happier every time he speaks to her.

"Mom, when do you plant the fall peas?" asks Charlie. "Is it almost time to do that?"

"In just a few weeks. *And*," says Mrs. Elliot, adding a

flourish to the word that Charlie can almost see, "we'll be able to do that together. I'm going to be coming home soon."

Mrs. Elliot is home in time to go to the fair with Charlie and his father. She climbs out of Susan's car, hair and eyes shining, looking cheerful and, Charlie thinks, maybe a bit plumper. He has just decided not to mention the plumpness when his mother, releasing him from a long hug, says, "Susan made me gain five pounds!" She laughs, and Charlie realizes he can't even remember the last time she laughed. Surely it was before RJ died.

Charlie's parents are holding hands now and smiling at each other and Charlie thinks his mother looks just like a girl, like one of the teenagers at the high school where he went once to see a play called *Our Town*.

Aunt Susan stays for the night. She plays catch in the yard with Charlie and Sunny and makes strawberry short-cake for dessert. Charlie, who has learned something about cooking this summer, makes a salad with vegetables from the garden, and when Aunt Susan tastes it she announces that it is stunning. Mrs. Elliot, who walked all around the garden with Charlie earlier in the afternoon, proclaims that the vegetables are the best ever and that Charlie must have the greenest thumb in the whole family.

"Next summer we can work on the garden together," says Charlie to his mother and she flashes her smile again. She flashes it once more when Charlie presents her with the stool at bedtime. "Mr. Hanna showed me what to do," he tells his mother, "but I did all the work myself with no help."

"This," says Mrs. Elliot, holding the stool in front of her and turning it around and around, "belongs in the living room, where everyone will be able to see it." She sets it in front of an armchair. "A place of honor," she says, and adds, "I feel like a queen with my very own personal footstool."

Before Charlie knows it, the county fair has come and gone (he and his parents go to it and Charlie wins a stuffed blue monkey by shooting at moving targets with a water pistol), and the start of school is just a day away.

Charlie and Sunny sit together on the front porch on that last evening of vacation, listening to the voices of Mr. and Mrs. Elliot in the kitchen as they clear the dinner dishes. Charlie strokes Sunny's muzzle, and then the baby soft fur behind her ears. "What are you going to do all day tomorrow without me?" he asks. Sunny squints her eyes and gazes at the horizon. "You keep Mom company, okay?" Charlie continues. "It'll be just you and her until I come home from school."

Charlie sits on the porch with Sunny until he can see fireflies winking among the fir trees, and his mother comes to the door and says, "Big day tomorrow, Charlie. Better get to bed early."

And so the summer ends and the autumn begins, and now the days seem more like they did a year ago, except that RJ is not a part of them. But somehow his absence feels less out of the ordinary than it did at the beginning of the summer. Maybe because RJ's chair at the kitchen table has been moved into the hallway, and some of the things in his room have been given away. RJ has not been forgotten, though. His photos, his trophies, even his sneakers and his report cards, garnish the farmhouse, but Charlie thinks these things seem like souvenirs of his life rather than remnants of it.

At the end of the first day of school, Charlie calls goodbye to Danny and to Mr. William, the ancient driver, and jumps down the steps of the bus to find his mother waiting at the end of their drive with Sunny. His mild humiliation over the presence of his mother (no other parents of fifthgraders were waiting to meet their children) is quickly erased by Sunny's exuberant greeting. She squats on the ground, tail sweeping the gravel, and when she can no longer stand it, she jumps to her feet and then straight up in the air before twirling around and landing with three short barks of joy. Nearly every kid on the bus sees Sunny and the next morning they all talk about her. Charlie is so lucky to have a dog like Sunny, they say. Sunny must be the best dog ever. They ask how she learned her tricks and what other things she can do.

When Mr. William deposits Charlie at his drive on the second afternoon, Sunny is waiting by herself. The third day of school is a half day, and to everyone's surprise, Sunny is waiting anyway. "How does she know when you're coming home?" Danny asks Charlie. "How did she know you'd be early?"

Charlie grins as he jumps down the bus steps. "It's just her way," he replies.

Charlie and Sunny run to the farmhouse and when Charlie enters the kitchen, he finds his mother standing at the stove, stirring and stirring something in a pot. She's staring at the wall over the stove, and as Charlie watches her, he realizes the fire isn't on under the pot. His mother is in some other place, and Charlie feels separated from that place by a great distance, as if he's looking at his mother through the wrong end of a telescope.

Charlie feels a hollowness in his stomach and knows his face is turning pale, but then his mother turns to him and says, "Guess what Sunny did today."

"What?" asks Charlie tentatively.

"She spent half the morning hiding her toys and the rest of the morning pretending to find them again."

Charlie laughs carefully. "Where did she hide them?"

"In all the places we hide them when we're playing with her. I think she was trying to amuse me."

"She's keeping you company," says Charlie, feeling more like himself again.

"And she's doing a good job of it." Mrs. Elliot smiles and it's her young girl's smile again.

Three weeks into September on a Saturday that is warm and humid but nevertheless carries the scents of autumn, Charlie and Sunny go for one of their walks in the woods. They haven't done this in a while, and Charlie takes great pleasure in packing a sandwich and a book and setting off with Sunny. "In a few weeks hunting season will begin," Charlie says, "and we'll have to stay close to home." He and Sunny find the flat rock that they like and Charlie spends the afternoon reading *The Twenty-One Balloons* while Sunny naps beside him.

They're on their way home—they'll be late for dinner if they don't hurry up—when Sunny lets out a yip and draws up short.

"What is it, girl?" asks Charlie. He bends down for a look and sees a wounded possum twitching in the leaves. "Leave it!" he commands Sunny, but Sunny leans in closer and picks up the possum in her jaws as gently as when she takes a snack from Charlie's fingers. She ignores Charlie's demands to drop the possum, and resolutely carries it, squirming, all the way back to the house.

"She rescued it!" Charlie exclaims to his parents.

"It's a good thing she decided to rescue a possum," says Mr. Elliot. "They aren't likely to carry rabies. Any other wild animal and this wouldn't be a good idea."

"Still, she rescued it," says Charlie. And he and his father nurse the possum back to health before Sunny's knowing eyes.

Autumn marches on and one day Charlie looks at the calendar and feels a prickle of concern. In a week RJ's birthday will be here; in a week RJ should be turning fourteen. Charlie watches his parents—especially his mother—closely, but their faces do not harden and his mother's laugh does not disappear, so Charlie relaxes. When RJ's birthday finally dawns, Charlie enters the kitchen uncertainly. He sees that his brother's chair is back at the table. "As a reminder," says his mother. "This day shouldn't go unnoticed."

Mrs. Elliot is quiet that day, and Mr. Elliot looks grim and stays longer at his job at the Daileys' farm than Charlie had expected. But that is all that happens. By the time Charlie goes to bed the chair has been replaced in the hall, and Charlie thinks, *We've had Thanksgiving and Christmas and Easter and graduation and the Fourth of July without RJ, and now his birthday has passed too.* Almost a year without RJ, only the first anniversary of his death left to observe in some way. When that day arrives, Charlie and his parents place flowers on RJ's grave in the cemetery, and Mr. and Mrs. Elliot cry briefly, but Charlie thinks his mother still looks robust and is relieved when, upon returning home, she reminds him to finish his homework and offers to go over his spelling list with him.

A year—a whole year—has now passed and somehow Charlie and his parents have walked through the dark woods and emerged into sunshine, Sunny at their sides.

11. BONE

After I left Mr. Bruce I ambled down the street, enjoying seeing close-up all the things that so far I had seen only from the windows of Franklin's apartment and the windows of his car. Here were buildings (Franklin called them stores) with people hurrying in and out of their doors. Here were lots of cars, some moving and some standing still. Here were people, here were dogs, here were trees, here were cats in doorways, here were buses and trucks and motorcycles. (Franklin called motorcycles "belching machines" and gave them a wide berth when he approached them in his car.)

What fun it was to be out among these things instead of looking at them through a pane of glass. I walked slowly, pausing frequently to sniff walls, sidewalks, trees, and fire hydrants. Each good long sniff told me a story, mostly about what other animals had visited the spot recently. I smelled dog, which was no surprise. I could see plenty of other dogs on the street, although they were all attached to leashes. I was the only one without a leash and a collar.

But I could also smell cat and squirrel and possum and something else rodent-like that I couldn't identify. This was very interesting.

After taking a particularly long sniff at the base of an oak tree, I wandered over to the store buildings. I poked my nose through any open doorways I found. Most of the doors were closed, though, and the people on the sidewalk who opened them stamped their feet and said, "It'll be good to get out of the cold."

I was about to pass yet another closed door when something caught the attention of my nose. It was a wonderful, tantalizing smell. I stuck my snout in the air and sniffed and sniffed. What was this place? I waited patiently by the door and hoped it would open, just as I had sat by Franklin's door, hoping it would open. I didn't have to wait long. Very soon a woman and two little girls walked by me, and the woman entered the store and held the door open for the girls. I scooted in behind them.

Oh, these odors were better than the ones at the garbage heap at the Merrions', or the kitchen at Thad and Isabel's, or the pet food store to which Franklin had taken me, or even the dump. Inside glass cases I could see loaves of bread, trays of cookies, and rows of buns and cakes. The air was warm and carried the scents of butter and sugar and spices.

If I couldn't live with Franklin, maybe I could live here.

I had just stepped up to one of the counters for a closer look at the things beyond the glass when a lady in an apron, who was loading even more goodies onto the shelves in the cases, called out in a very loud voice, "No dogs allowed! Please take your dog out of here. This is a food establishment."

The woman and the girls and several other people looked around and around until the lady in the apron said, this time more loudly, "Ma'am? Your dog?"

The woman who had let me into the store said, "Me? That isn't my dog."

"Well, whose is it?"

When nobody said anything, the loud lady hustled around in front of the counter. "Let's see where you belong, dog," she said, and reached for the place where my collar should have been. She frowned. "Hmm. No collar. I suppose I should call somebody. You come here with me." She tried to pull me behind the counter, but her hands did not feel gentle, and suddenly, as much as I wanted a piece of cake or a loaf of bread, I bolted toward the door. To my surprise it opened just as I reached it, and I squeezed my way past a family who were entering the bakery, and streaked down the street.

I didn't stop running until I reached what looked like the last of the store buildings. It was set apart from the others, and although I couldn't catch any good scents wafting from it, I was hopeful that someone inside might offer me food or water. So I stood on my hind legs and gazed through the window. I could see shelves and counters holding small, glittery things like the ornaments Isabel wore on her fingers and wrists and ears and around her neck. A young man, very thin with wispy hair and a frown between his eyes, was sitting in a chair holding a book. He was the only one in the building. He glanced at me, then looked back at his book. When he glanced up again a bit later and saw that I was still gazing at him through the window, he slammed the book down and opened the door in a way that reminded me of George the morning he threw Squirrel and me out of the car.

"Go on! Get!" he said, and he leaned over and swatted my rump with his book.

I was very thirsty and had hoped that maybe I would find a bowl of water on his floor, but now I ran away from the man. I ran until I reached a corner, then I turned the corner and kept running until the store buildings were far behind me. The sky was beginning to grow dark and my paws were cold. I hadn't noticed the cold on my brief jaunts into Franklin's yard to pee, or on the short walk from Franklin's apartment to his car, but now it seeped into the pads on the bottoms of my feet. I stood still for a bit and lifted my paws off the icy ground one at a time, but I didn't feel any warmer. The wind was blowing now, rushing around me like Estelle the cat chasing her tail, and I began to shiver.

I walked along a dark street, passing houses with lighted windows. I thought about trying to get inside one of the houses, but the memory of the man with the book was fresh, and so I kept walking and shivering, feeling my tongue grow dry and my belly start to rumble. When I reached what seemed to be the last house on the road I noticed a dish on the front stoop. Cautiously, I approached it. It was full of water. I took a long drink, but then I left the house behind and walked until I reached woods. I found that in the woods there were no streetlights, no lights at all; nothing but trees and black blackness and me.

I spent the night in those woods. I had never spent an entire night outdoors. At the Merrions', Squirrel and I had slept in the shed, and after that I had been an indoor dog. But now I was outdoors and alone. And very, very cold. I tucked my nose under my tail. I pulled my feet to my belly. But my ears stung and I trembled and shook. And I heard nighttime sounds that kept me wakeful until the first rays of sunshine shimmered among the branches of the trees. I had been very aware that I was separated from the owls and raccoons and skunks, from the coyotes and fishers and other stray dogs, by the black blackness only, and that was no protection.

In the morning, at first light, I rose to my feet and set off. I did not want to stay in the woods, so I followed my own scent (noting especially the spots where I had stopped to pee the day before) back to the road with the houses. Once I reached the houses, though, I didn't know where to go.

I began to feel nervous and soon I was running up and down the same street, back and forth, back and forth. I sniffed and ran and turned around and sniffed and ran and turned around again. I was panting, and my belly was emptier than it had ever, ever been.

I heard a car on the street behind me and I scurried along the sidewalk and then across a lawn toward a house. I watched the car from a distance. It slowed down and stopped.

"Come here, pooch!" A woman opened the car door and leaned out, extending her hand to me. "Here, pooch! Come here. I won't hurt you."

I backed even farther away. And then I smelled meat. Turkey? Hamburger? I wasn't sure and I didn't care. I started to drool.

"Come here, pooch," said the woman again, and I realized that the meat was in her hand.

I took several steps toward the car.

"Good boy. Come on."

I took several more steps.

When I was very near to the woman she held her hand

even closer to me. Tentatively I stretched my neck forward. And suddenly the meat was on the ground and the woman's hands were grasping my front legs.

In a flash I pulled free and ran as fast as I could between two houses and away from the road.

"Come back!" the woman called. "I want to help you. I know you're lost."

It wasn't easy to run fast with no food in my belly, but I didn't stop until I was far, far from the houses. Then I walked and walked and walked. It was later, when the weak sun was at its highest point in the sky, that I found the stream. It ran out from some woods, under a road, and along a field toward a house that stood all by itself in a grove of trees.

I stepped carefully down the bank to the water and took a long drink. After that I followed the stream. I followed it to the house. I didn't want to go into the woods again. I didn't want to meet any more people either, but I thought maybe I would find a garbage heap by the house.

I didn't find a garbage heap, but I did find garbage. It was in a metal can like the ones in the yard behind Franklin's apartment. Those cans were topped off with lids that Mr. Bruce kept tightly in place. The lid on this can was loose and I knocked it off easily. Then I tipped over the can and inside ... inside were the ends of a loaf of bread and some pieces of dry ham and a mouthful of cooked eggs, enough food to fill me up nicely. There were other things too, things that were not meant to be eaten, but I pawed them aside and concentrated on the food.

All this took a while and I stopped frequently to look around me and to listen carefully. No people came out of the house, though, or drove close to me in a car. Even so, I decided to leave after I had finished eating. I trotted back to the stream and continued to follow it. When the sky grew dark at the end of the day I came to another house in the country. I slept in the shelter of a stone wall at the edge of the yard. The next morning I ate a nice breakfast from a bowl of crunchy food on the patio behind the house. I don't know who the food was meant for, but I was too hungry to care. When I had licked the bowl clean I hurried away from the house.

This was the beginning of my time of wandering. I wandered from house to house and town to town while the cold air nipped at the tips of my ears and the snows fell and covered the ground. I wandered while the air grew warm again and the leaves returned to the trees and the outside animals had their babies. I wandered while the warm air grew hot and then very hot and sometimes water was hard to find.

I never stayed long in one place. A night or two, a week or two, and it was time to move on. Finding garbage and eating it secretly and quickly became easier. Occasionally I caught small animals in the woods and made a meal of them, but I didn't like the woods much. I was a country dog and a town dog, but not a woods dog.

The air was growing cool again and the leaves on the trees had a different look to them and were starting to fall to the ground when I emerged from a grassy meadow one afternoon, found myself at the side of a road, and came to an abrupt stop. I had been to this place before. I was sure of it. The smells were familiar. Not recently familiar, but familiar from some time in the past.

I sniffed. I sniffed the air and the ground and then the air again.

Something told me to cross the road, so I did, after listening for cars first. When I reached the other side, I followed the road for a while and then when I reached a particular lane leading from the road, I turned and followed that.

This place, wherever I was, felt like a home. But I wasn't on the road to George and Marcy's house (which hadn't felt like a home anyway), and I wasn't on any of the streets around Thad and Isabel's house or Franklin's apartment building. They had lived in towns and I was in the country, and the smells here were different from town smells, but familiar all the same.

Sniff, sniff, sniff. From the many smells in the air I

selected several that I knew well: cat (but not Estelle), bird (especially barn swallow), and boy. My heart quickened and so did my pace. I trotted along and when I came to a stone wall, my pace quickened even further so that I reached the garbage heap in no time. I was so excited that I didn't notice that nothing in the heap was fresh. Instead I loped on through the woods until I came to the shed. It stood before me with its open window, the door still ajar. And even as I watched the shed, the face of a young cat, a tabby with black stripes along his forehead, peered around the door and surveyed the yard before heading across it in a purposeful way.

I had stumbled across the Merrions' property.

Back then, back when I accidentally returned to the Merrions', I didn't know the names of the seasons. Now I do, and I can say that Squirrel and I had left this place at the end of a summer, and that I had been away from it for the autumn, the winter, the spring, the summer, the next autumn, the next winter, the next spring, the next summer, and that now it was autumn again.

The yard looked largely the same as it had on the day Squirrel and I walked away from it, except that it was wearing its autumn face, a face I had never seen, since Squirrel and I had lived at the Merrions' for only two seasons— spring and summer. There were the gardens, as carefully tended as always, but barer now, with more earth showing, the summer plants beginning to die back. There was the swing the Merrion children used to ride on. There was the driveway, although no car was parked on it.

No car, and the property was quiet except for outdoor autumn sounds. The Merrions were not here.

I trotted from the woods and poked my snout through the door to the shed. There were the flowerpots, the wheelbarrow, and the old nesting boxes, still inhabited, I saw at once, by cats. Several of them hissed at me. They didn't know me and I didn't know them. I backed out.

I sat in the yard. The Merrions' yard was pleasant when no Merrions were in it. But then I checked the garbage heap and found only the remains of old things; nothing I could eat.

I went to sleep with an empty belly that evening. I slept in the shed, very near the door, which was how I happened to hear the Merrions' car as soon as it turned onto their drive. I had been asleep for just a short while when my ears picked up the sound of the tires on the pavement. I got to my feet and peered through the door.

And there they were, spilling out of their car in the glow of several outdoor lights: the Merrion parents, the older boy, the girl, and Matthias. Matthias was much larger than he had been the last time I'd seen him. His legs were long and I saw that he walked more quickly. He lifted things out of the car and set them on the drive, and the very last thing he lifted out was a fluffy white dog with poofs of fur around her legs and on top of her head.

"Good girl," Matthias said to her when she ambled over to the lawn and squatted to pee. "Good girl, Princess." Then Matthias picked her up, cradling her in his arms, and carried her into the house.

The Merrions' yard grew quiet again. In the morning I left it without even bothering to check the garbage heap.

A few days later, after more wandering, more hiding, more eating from trash cans, I came to the top of a small mountain. I sat down for a rest and noticed that a little town had grown up in the valley between this mountain and another one not far away. Many of the streets in the town ran from mountain to mountain. I could see the roofs of houses dotting those streets. Rooftops, treetops, a sleepy-looking town, and maybe one with lots of garbage.

Food in the town and good hiding places just outside of the town. This looked like a place for me.

12. HENRY

Henry thought that for the rest of his life he would remember the first time he saw the tan dog. It was on an autumn day so clear and lovely that the weather was the first thing anyone mentioned when starting a conversation. The newscaster on the radio program that Henry and his parents listened to while they ate their breakfast even called that Thursday one of the ten best days of the year. The air was cool, the sun shone brilliantly, and when Henry walked to school that morning and tipped his head back to gaze through the branches of the maple trees, the red and yellow and orange leaves against the deep blue of the sky reminded him of the crazy quilt his father's aunt had made the year Henry was born.

Henry walked along by himself and tried to forget how mad he was at his parents. But he *was* mad—too mad to walk through town with either one of them, and so he slogged along Tinker Lane, weighed down by his full backpack and his angry thoughts, and looked at the familiar early morning sights. There was the big old house with the bird feeders and the birdhouse and the birdbath, but no sign of an occupant. There was the little school bus picking up Mackey Brannigan's sister. There were Antony and Owen and the pack of kids who always walked to school together. They were turning the corner onto Nassau Street.

Henry was just thinking that maybe he ought to run to catch up with them when out of the corner of his eye he spotted movement where there should be no movement. He swiveled his head to the right and saw three garbage cans in the narrow yard between two houses a block from Nassau. Henry stared at the cans. He stared at the yard and the houses on either side of it. Nothing was moving. He looked at the cans again. And a slender tan paw appeared between two of them, reaching delicately, followed by a scruffy tan head.

Henry came to a stop. "Hey," he whispered.

As he watched, the dog tentatively squeezed the rest of his body between the cans, then turned, stood on his hind legs, and began to explore the lids of the cans with his front paws and his snout.

Henry held his breath. Who was this dog? He wasn't wearing a collar, and he didn't look cared for. Henry could see the outlines of ribs under his fur. And the dog was dirty. He was so dirty, in fact, that Henry wasn't even sure he was tan. Maybe he was white and needed a very thorough bath.

"Dog?" said Henry curiously.

He had spoken quietly, but in an instant the dog dropped to the ground and spun around. When he caught sight of Henry, he shot back between the cans and disappeared.

"Well," said Henry in a louder voice. "This is interesting."

Henry didn't see the dog again until Saturday. He was spending the afternoon in a solitary fashion, wandering the roads of Claremont the way he used to do with Matthew. He *had* been spending the day indoors until his mother had clucked her tongue and told him to please go outside and not waste the sunshine. So Henry had made the rounds of the stores on Nassau Street, and now he was walking along the alley behind them to see what he might find there. (He and Matthew had once come across a lone sneaker in perfectly good condition, and another time Matthew had pounced on four one-dollar bills wadded up in a dried-out rubber band.) Henry leaned over to examine something shiny by the back door of the jewelry store (it turned out to be a gum wrapper), and when he straightened up he found himself face-to-face with the scruffy dog, who had just peered suspiciously around the corner of the alley.

Henry, who had thought he was alone, let out a shout,

the dog barked shrilly, and Henry ran back to Nassau Street while the dog took off in the other direction. When Henry had recovered, he returned to the alley, but found it deserted.

"Dog?" called Henry. "Boy?" He was fairly certain the dog was a male. "Come here, boy. . . . Where did you go?"

Despite his scare, Henry took this encounter as a good sign. He had now spotted the dog twice—and not hanging around the edges of town, where in the past he had spotted stray dogs from time to time, but right *in* town, and right in Henry's own neighborhood.

Henry made a deal with himself. If he saw the dog again, then he would find a way to convince his parents to let him keep him. Maybe they would say okay to a *free* dog. After all, one of their objections to getting a dog was the expense involved. But if Henry presented them with this stray, then they wouldn't have to pay an adoption fee. Furthermore (Henry began to smile as his idea took shape), if Henry could teach the dog some manners and housebreak him before his mother and father met him, then Henry could say, "And we don't even need to train him. I already took care of that."

Henry didn't have to wait long to see the dog again. He spotted him later that very afternoon. The dog was back on Tinker Lane, nosing around someone else's garbage cans.

"Hello, boy!" called Henry, and this time the dog paused

and watched Henry with his solemn brown eyes for several seconds before disappearing behind the trash cans.

Henry put on speed as he ran toward his house. True to his word, he headed straight for his bedroom to draw up a plan for training the dog, *his* dog.

"I'm going to do my homework now," Henry called to his mother, certain she wouldn't tell him to go back outside if she thought he was starting his weekend assignments.

He closed his door, sat at his desk, and removed a large pad of paper from the drawer. He found a pen, thought for a moment, then headed the top sheet of paper: *REHABILITATION PLAN.*

How, wondered Henry, was he to take the pup from a wary, unwashed stray to a friendly, attractive, well-trained dog, fit to be a family pet? One day at a time, that was how. And so he drew up his plan:

Day 1—approach dog and allow him to sniff hand

Day 2—pat dog

Day 3—attempt to hug dog

Day 4—tell dog his new name (Buddy)

Day 5—call Buddy and give him a cookie when he comes

Day 6—teach Buddy to sit

Henry wasn't sure how step 6 was to be accomplished, but he was reasonably certain that he could find a book on dog training in the library.

Day 7—teach Buddy to do something that will im-press Mom and Dad

Day 8—teach Buddy how to walk on a leash (make sure to buy a collar and a leash first)

Henry glanced across the room at his dresser, on which sat his wallet.

Day 9—give Buddy a bath

Day 10—make sure Buddy is housebroken.

Henry was particularly uncertain about this last step. How would he know if Buddy was housebroken without first bringing him inside the house? And he knew that Buddy must remain a secret outdoor dog until the entire rehabili-tation plan had been accomplished.

Still, the plan was very exciting. In just ten days—less than two weeks from now—Henry would have a fully trained, friendly, and clean dog. He didn't expect to see Buddy again until the next day (that would be asking for too much), but he could still start on his plan, and the first thing he needed to do was count the money in his wallet to see if he had enough to buy a collar and a leash and also some dog treats. This was when Henry remembered that he had rashly decided to donate his money to the animal shelter and that it was not in his wallet but stuffed into the enve-lope that his mother had put somewhere in the kitchen. Well, too bad. Henry needed that money now. His original plan hadn't worked, but this one would. Henry could make a donation to the shelter some other time. He crept into the kitchen, found the envelope, and tiptoed back to his room with it. He dumped the money on his bed and counted it. Yes, he had enough for a collar, a leash, and treats, with a fair amount left over.

"I'm going back to town!" Henry called a few minutes later as he dashed down the stairs.

"Now? It's almost dinnertime," his mother replied.

"I'll be quick," said Henry. And he was. He made a hurried trip to the pet supply store, and then checked two books on dog training out of the public library. As he did so, he crossed his fingers, hoping that Ms. Delacroix, the librarian on duty, wouldn't mention the books to his father. Books on dog training might raise eyebrows, and Henry didn't want his father to become suspicious. He ran home and stashed the books, his purchases, and the rehabilitation plan under his bed.

The next morning, Henry awoke with a delicious feeling of anticipation in his stomach. It was time to begin his plan. Even though he had already memorized every step of it, he pulled the plan from beneath his bed and read, "Day One—approach dog and allow him to sniff hand." He returned the plan to its hiding place. "Okay. That's what I'll do today," said Henry. And he decided it might be a good idea to do it more than once in order to let Buddy become familiar with him. As an afterthought, Henry stuffed the bag of treats in his pocket. It couldn't hurt to reward Buddy after he had been brave enough to sniff Henry's hand.

Henry headed outside early that morning. He found that the day was not as nice as the previous one had been. There was a chill in the air, and a damp fog had settled over Claremont. It curled around the houses and trees on Tinker Lane like steam rising from a bowl of soup. The fog was not going to make finding Buddy any easier, but Henry was determined to stay on schedule with the Rehabilitation Plan.

He walked slowly across his yard and turned right when he reached the sidewalk. It had been a while since he had been outdoors so early on a Sunday morning, and Henry was surprised by how quiet Tinker Lane was. "Buddy!" Henry called softly, and then he realized that the tan dog didn't know his name yet. "Here, boy!" he called. "Here, boy! Come get a treat!"

Henry heard all sorts of gentle autumn noises, but no dog noises. He heard wet leaves falling to the ground, and a crow cawing in the distance, and the rustle of chrysanthemums and yellowing ferns stirred by the breeze. But he did not hear any barking or yipping or whining. Henry crossed the street and soon another sound reached his ears—a soft tinkling, like a musical instrument.

The tinkling sound grew louder and at the same time the fog shifted and suddenly the lavender house belonging to the person Henry never saw gradually appeared, as if a magician had lifted a scarf. Henry realized that the sound came from a ring of metal chimes hanging from the branch of a tree. Henry stopped and stared at the yard— and jumped when a timid voice said, "Hello."

Henry scanned the yard.

"I'm over here," said the voice. "I'm hard to see in the fog."

Henry continued to stare, and finally made out a tiny woman carrying a bucket of birdseed. "Oh," said Henry. "Hello." And then, because he didn't know what else to say, he asked, "Have you seen a dog?"

The woman set down her bucket. "You're Henry, aren't you?"

"I—" said Henry.

"I didn't know you had a dog."

Henry was surprised this woman knew anything about him at all. "Well," he said at last, "I don't. But I've seen one around here. A stray. And I wanted to . . ." He paused. How much should he tell this woman? "I just wanted to give him some food."

"Oh, the tan dog?" said the woman. "That scruffy one? The one that looks like a golden retriever? I saw him yesterday."

"But not today?" asked Henry, disappointed.

"No, not today."

"Oh."

"I know he'll appreciate some food," the woman went on. "That's very thoughtful of you."

"Thanks," said Henry. He started off down the sidewalk again, then stopped and turned around. "How did you know my name?" he asked the woman, privately thinking, *Don't be a witch, don't be a witch.*

"I know everyone on Tinker Lane," she replied. "I've lived here longer than anyone else. My name is Letty Lewis," she added. She poured birdseed into a feeder hanging from a tree. "You'd like that stray dog for yourself, wouldn't you?" she asked. "But your parents have probably said you can't have a dog. That's like parents. Just like them. Exactly the kind of thing parents would say."

So she was a witch after all. Henry backed away.

"You probably have a plan for keeping the dog somehow," Letty Lewis went on. "Well, that's very sensible of you. I'll keep my eye out for him and let you know if I see him. I could tell you when you're on your way to school tomorrow morning. Or on your way home."

"Okay," replied Henry. "Thanks." As he set off down the street again, he said over his shoulder, "Letty Lewis? The dog's name is Buddy."

Henry searched for Buddy most of that day and didn't see him, so he decided to start the Rehabilitation Plan over from scratch on Monday. As soon as he returned home from school he set out from his backyard and walked through one backyard after another, calling for Buddy and fingering the treats in his pocket. He was nearing Mountain View when he crossed through yet another yard and realized he wasn't alone. He heard voices above his head and looked up to see an elaborate tree house, a pair of legs dangling from the doorway. The legs, which were attached to a boy, scrambled down a ladder as fast as a monkey, and jumped to the ground. They were followed by four more scrambling pairs of legs. Henry found himself facing Antony, and two boys and two girls who looked very much like Antony.

One of the boys, small and fierce, who was wearing a pirate's hat, glared at Henry and said, "State your business here, matey!"

"Peter," said Antony, "that's enough. This is Henry. He lives down the street. Hi, Henry."

"Hi," Henry replied. "Have you seen a dog?"

"What kind of dog?" asked one of the girls.

"A tan one. Who doesn't have a home."

The girl clutched at her heart. "Oh. A homeless dog. That is the saddest thing I ever heard."

Antony rolled his eyes. "I saw a tan dog a couple of

days ago. He was over in Owen's yard. Why are you looking for him?"

"I just . . . want to feed him."

"We could help you find him," said Antony. "These are
my brothers and sisters," he added. "Peter, Sal—"

"I'm Sal," said the smallest boy. "It's short for Salvatore."

"Sofia and Ginny," Antony finished.

"Really?" said Henry. "You'll help me?"

"Sure."

Henry and Antony and Antony's brothers and sisters
looked and looked for Buddy that afternoon, but by suppertime they had not seen him.

"Not his hide nor one single hair," said Sofia, the dra-
matic sister.

The next morning Henry set out along Tinker Lane and
saw Owen and Antony and the group of kids ahead. He now
knew that the other kids were Sofia and Ginny and Peter
and Sal. They were standing in a bunch at the end of Owen's
driveway.

"Henry!" called Sal. "Look what we brought you!"
He withdrew two cans of dog food from his backpack. "We
thought maybe if you left the food out, the dog would come
to *you*."

Now, why hadn't Henry thought of that? "Thanks,"
he said, slipping the cans into his own backpack. "That's a

great idea." And then, as if he had done so every day of his life, Henry walked to Claremont Elementary with Owen and Antony and the others. The Rehabilitation Plan was several days off schedule, but Henry wasn't too concerned. Something interesting was happening on Tinker Lane.

13. CHARLIE

*B*ang!

From the end of Charlie's bed, Sunny lets out a whimper.

Charlie, groggy with sleep, reaches down to pat her. "It's okay," he tells her. "It's just a hunter, and he's not even nearby. I know you don't like the gunshots, but we can't do anything about them."

Sunny has never liked loud noises. She jumps if a door slams or if the television comes on too loudly. She's miserable during thunderstorms. And now it's hunting season again.

"Darn old hunters," mutters Charlie from under his covers. They're scaring Sunny and ruining Charlie's Saturday, on which he has planned to sleep late.

Bang! Bang!

Sunny slinks across the bed, tail between her legs, dark eyes even darker with alarm, and paws desperately at the covers. Charlie lifts them for her and she burrows underneath and presses herself hotly against his stomach.

"Poor old girl," murmurs Charlie.

After several more shotgun blasts, Charlie knows he won't be able to go back to sleep, so he slides out of bed and peers at the clock. "It's after nine, Sunny," he announces. "We might as well get up."

Charlie, shadowed by Sunny, pads into the kitchen. He finds his mother there, removing serving dishes from the cupboards and setting them on the table, which is already crowded with plates, ladles, recipe cards, tins of spices, a turkey baster, and the Elliots' Thanksgiving platter, the one with the cornucopia painted in the center.

"Morning, sleepyhead," Mrs. Elliot greets Charlie. "You slept late."

"Until the hunters started shooting," Charlie replies, and yawns. "What's all this?"

"Just five days until Thanksgiving. I have to start getting ready. Aunt Susan and everyone will be arriving on Tuesday. I have a lot to do before then."

His mother, humming, returns to her work, and Charlie thinks about Thanksgiving as he fixes himself a bowl of cereal. They didn't celebrate it the year before. RJ had been buried just several weeks earlier, and Mr. and Mrs. Elliot never mentioned the holiday, although Charlie knew they thought about it all that Thursday as they went silently about their chores. His father spent the afternoon working in the barn and his mother began to answer the condolence notes that had been arriving in the mail. Every day she'd sorted through the letters, slicing the envelopes carefully with a silver letter opener, reading the notes, and then placing them tidily in stacks on a tray in the kitchen. The stacks had grown into towers, which began to teeter, and Mr. Elliot eyed them at breakfast on Thanksgiving. Nothing was said about the towers, but as soon as Mr. Elliot disappeared into the barn, Mrs. Elliot found her fountain pen and her best stationery, sat down at the table, and reached for a note on top of one of the piles. She didn't stop writing until it was time to go to bed and Thanksgiving was mercifully over.

But now, a year later, Mrs. Elliot is humming and planning and poring through cookbooks. "Charlie," she says, "I'm feeling festive. See if you can find some Christmas music on the radio."

Charlie fiddles with the dial, but the best he can come up with is a recording of the previous year's Thanksgiving service at a church in Chicago. "That's nice. Leave it there," says his mother, who begins singing, "We shall come rejoicing, bringing in the sheaves," in her low voice.

Charlie eats his breakfast sitting on a stool at the kitchen counter since the table is so crowded with the beginnings of Thanksgiving dinner. He gazes out the window, listening to the distant gunshots. The morning is raw and overcast.

"You'd think the hunters would stay home on a day like this," he says crabbily to his mother.

She gives him a rueful smile. "You just have to get through it," she replies, and Charlie knows she means hunting season.

"Well, I don't understand why the hunters have to go out there and kill for sport. For *sport*. It would be one thing if they actually *needed* the animals they shoot. You know, to make coats or whatever. But they don't. And half the time, they don't even *eat* what they kill. Like with deer, they just cut off their heads and hang them in their living rooms. How would a hunter like it if a deer came around and cut off the head of someone in the hunter's family just so he could hang it over his mantelpiece and say, 'Look! I was finally able to add a twenty-two-year-old man to my collection.'"

"Charlie!" Mrs. Elliot is trying not to laugh and also doesn't want to get caught up in this discussion that she and Charlie have had many, many times in the past. She glances at her watch. "Honey," she says, "it's still early. Don't waste this day being angry. Why don't you give me a hand in the kitchen? Or make place cards for Thursday. That would be helpful."

"Mom. I'm not seven," says Charlie, imagining himself crayoning turkeys and Pilgrims on construction paper. He finishes his cereal and sets his bowl in the sink. "I think I'll take a walk with Sunny."

"All right. But stay out of the woods on our property," replies Mrs. Elliot over the sound of another gunshot. "I don't want you in the woods until hunting season is over. And wear something bright red."

The flat rock, on which Charlie and Sunny have shared many picnics, is not on the Elliots' property, and anyway the day is too cold for picnics or for sitting outside and reading. In fact, Charlie notes with satisfaction, the air feels cold enough for snow. Maybe the first snow will fall on Thanksgiving Day. Maybe they'll have a white Thanksgiving this year and a white Christmas too.

Charlie and Sunny set out for a walk around the Elliots' yard. Charlie stands for a while considering the vegetable garden. In one corner he and his mother have already planted garlic cloves, which will sprout early the next spring. Not much else remains—a few tangled vines from the winter squash and some very resistant crabgrass. Charlie pulls these up and tosses them onto a brush heap nearby. The day is now growing foggy and Charlie realizes that he hasn't heard gunshots for half an hour or so. "Good," he says aloud to Sunny. "Maybe the murderers have all gone home."

Sunny, who is sitting neatly at the edge of the garden, front feet lined up perfectly and her tail sticking out straight behind her, tilts her head and gives Charlie a grin, and this makes Charlie laugh.

*   *   *

141

After lunch, which the Elliots eat hastily so that Mrs. Elliot can get back to her preparations, Charlie's father says to him, "Can you come help me with something in the barn?" There's a look on his face that Charlie can't quite read. Secretive? Amused? Mysterious? Conspiratorial?

"Okay," replies Charlie, intrigued.

Charlie and Sunny follow Mr. Elliot to the barn. They walk past scattering, clucking hens, past the stacks of painting supplies, past the makeshift office, to a stall near the back wall. Mr. Elliot steps aside so Charlie can enter the stall first, and Charlie sees something large perched on a workbench. The something is covered with a sheet.

"What is it?" asks Charlie.

His father lifts the sheet. "I'm making it for your mother for Christmas."

"Is it . . . a dollhouse?"

His father nods. "It's going to be."

"It's really great, Dad, but Mom is . . ." He pauses. How to say this delicately? "Mom's a grown-up."

Mr. Elliot smiles. "I know. But she's always wanted a dollhouse. And look." He shows Charlie a sheaf of papers. They're plans for an elaborate Victorian house, complete with a gabled roof, gingerbread trim, and window boxes. "I know she'll like this. Even if she is a grown-up. She'll have fun decorating it and making furniture for it. The only thing is that I'm not sure I can finish it on time. Not without help.

Would you like to help me? You did such a good job making the stool last summer."

If a dollhouse is something his mother really wants, then Charlie is happy to work on it. Plus, he likes the idea of a Christmas secret in the barn. "Okay," he says. "Sure. But you'll have to show me what to do."

Charlie and his father work until Charlie realizes that outside the light is starting to fade, and also that he hasn't seen Sunny in quite some time.

"When did Sunny leave?" he asks.

"I'm not sure," his father replies, his eyes on the plans.

"I'd better go find her," says Charlie. "I want to know where she is."

Charlie walks across the yard to the farmhouse. "Mom? Did Sunny come in?"

"No," calls Mrs. Elliot from the kitchen. "I thought she was with you."

Charlie walks through the house anyway, calling for Sunny, but his mother is right. She isn't there.

He stands in the yard and looks in all directions. The fog has lifted, but he still can't see very far in the late afternoon light.

"Sunny! Sunny!" calls Charlie. He listens for a bark or for the sound of her muscular body crashing through the underbrush.

Nothing.

"Sunny? . . . *Sunny!*"

This has happened before. Sunny doesn't come right away and Charlie envisions all sorts of awful things that might have happened to her. Then, finally, Sunny comes flying to him from the far reaches of their property, looking as though she has a good story to tell.

Charlie begins to walk through the field. "Sunny! Sunny! Suuuunny!"

"Charlie?" Mr. Elliot is jogging through the field behind him. "Haven't you found her yet?"

Charlie is now feeling very nervous and his nervousness is making him cross, which is why he almost says to his father, "If I'd found her, why would I be calling her?" But instead he says breathlessly, "No. Not yet. I haven't seen her or heard her and she isn't in the house."

"We'll find her, son," says Mr. Elliot, and despite his fears, Charlie warms at the sound of the word *son*.

Charlie and his father decide to separate so that they can each walk along one side of their property, at the edge of the woods.

"Sunny! Here, girl!" calls Mr. Elliot.

"Come, Sunny!" calls Charlie. He would like to look in the woods too, but remembers his mother's warning about hunters.

And finally, when Charlie thinks he can bear the search no longer, he spots Sunny far ahead. In the dim light he can just see that her rump is in the air, her front legs scrabbling

excitedly in the brush. She has found something enticing—
a mouse or a mole or a vole—and she is determined to
claim it for herself.

"Sunny!" Charlie cries with relief. Then, "Dad! I see her!
She's way over there." He waves his arms in the air and
points ahead to Sunny's wiggling rump.

Charlie begins to run, and Mr. Elliot crosses the field at
a good clip, his long legs pumping the way they must have
done years ago when he was a star on the Monroe County
High School football team.

"SUNNY!" Charlie shouts in his loudest voice possible,
and finally, *finally,* Sunny hears him. She raises her head—
she has not caught her prize after all—turns, and lopes to
ward Charlie. Her doggie grin is in place. She has had an
enjoyable afternoon.

Charlie and Sunny are not twenty feet apart when a
gunshot sounds, this one very close by, and Sunny jumps,
all four feet off the ground.

"It's okay, Sunny," Charlie says, still running toward her.
"Just a loud noise, remember?"

But Sunny has landed in a heap and doesn't move.

Charlie falters. He feels his father by his side.

"Stop right here," says Mr. Elliot, placing his hand on
Charlie's shoulder.

Charlie ignores him. He shrugs away and runs to
Sunny, calling, "Get up! Get up *now.*"

Sunny is lying very still, more still even than when she

sleeps. Charlie stoops and turns her over gently. His hands come away slick with blood.

"No!" Charlie shouts. "No! Dad!" He peers through the trees. A hunter must be close by. "Stupid idiot! Stupid idiot! Dad, some stupid idiot hunter was shooting onto our *property*. That's illegal. Stupid idiot," he says again, and he's whispering now, stroking Sunny's lovely snout, her silky ears.

Charlie hears a rustling, ever so faint, farther off in the field, and he jerks his head up. He can just make out a figure. Someone is walking slowly, very slowly and carefully, toward Charlie and Sunny from the direction of the Elliots' house, a shadowy object cradled in one arm.

"Go away!" Charlie yells, but the figure keeps coming until finally Charlie can make out Mr. Hanna's destroyed face. Charlie is on his feet in seconds and he rushes toward the old man. "Murderer, murderer! You murdered Sunny."

Mr. Hanna shakes his head, but he can't speak. He kneels by Sunny. His mouth is trembling and his eyes leak tears. Charlie raises his fist. Maybe he would have hit Mr. Hanna and maybe not, but before he can find out, his father's hands grab him from behind and pull him backward, and it's at that moment that they all hear the sound of someone running—crashing—through the woods, running away from what he has caused. And Charlie sees that Mr. Hanna isn't carrying his gun. He's carrying a sack of apples, which, Charlie finds out later, he was bringing to the Elliots as a Thanksgiving gift.

Mr. Hanna has dropped the bag and now he traces his hand down Sunny's graceful body, stroking her slowly all the way from her ears to her tail.

Charlie doesn't know what to do; has absolutely no idea. He wants to apologize to Mr. Hanna, but he can't find his voice. He wants to take off into the woods after the hunter, but as soon as he steps toward the trees, his father puts his hands on his shoulders and turns him around.

Charlie falls to his knees. "I want her back!" he cries. He begins to sob. "I want *him* back."

Mr. Elliot sits on the ground beside Charlie and puts his arm around him and they both cry quietly while Mr. Hanna moves his hand up to Sunny's head again and begins another slow stroke along her body down to her tail.

The next morning, Charlie and his parents bury Sunny among the fir trees at the exact spot where RJ landed after he fell.

14. HENRY

Henry didn't want to say that his Rehabilitation Plan had failed, but if he thought about things for as long as two seconds, he had to admit that that was pretty much what had happened: The plan had fallen flat. If it were a school assignment, Henry's grade would have been a large red *D*.

During the weeks that followed, as fall had turned to winter, Henry had spent hours scouring Claremont, calling, "Buddy! Buddy!" Frequently, he came across Buddy, but he couldn't say that the dog actually knew his name. What Buddy did know was that when he saw Henry running toward him calling, "Buddy!" and holding an outstretched hand in his direction, that hand held food or treats. Buddy was now comfortable enough to take the treats from the hand—and even to allow Henry to pat him—before he ran off to eat in private.

So. What had Henry accomplished? He was fairly sure he had accomplished Day 1 of his plan, since Buddy definitely allowed Henry to approach him and occasionally he sniffed his hand before snatching the treats. Day 2, since Buddy also permitted Henry to pat him. And *maybe*, Henry decided, he had accomplished part of Day 4, since Buddy had certainly heard his name called often enough. And he had sort of accomplished Day 5. But what about "Hug dog," which was supposed to have been accomplished before Day 4? And what about everything after Day 4? The leash and collar Henry had secretly bought still lay coiled, brightly colored and new smelling, under his bed. Buddy couldn't sit or do tricks, Henry hadn't given him a bath, and he still had no idea whether Buddy was housebroken. (He preferred not to think about that. Better to concentrate on other things.)

One day when Henry and Owen and Antony and Antony's brothers and sisters were walking to school, Sofia said, "We're going to decorate our tree tonight!"

"Our *outside* tree," said Ginny importantly. "We don't have an inside tree yet."

Henry stopped in his tracks. Christmas trees! What had happened to the long, long autumn—the one that had boringly stretched in front of him after Matthew had moved away? Where had it gone? Halloween was over, Thanksgiving was over, and now Christmas was almost here. Henry had been so caught up in Buddy's Rehabilitation Plan that the days and weeks and months had sped past.

"What's the matter?" asked Owen, turning around to look at Henry.

"Nothing." Henry ran to catch up with the kids. "I was just thinking. There are only thirteen days until Christmas."

Henry didn't know whether to be excited or disappointed.

Henry's parents brought the boxes of Christmas decorations down from the attic. His mother arrayed angels and elves and snow globes and miniature trees along the mantelpiece. His father twined strands of tiny gold lights through ropes of pine branches and arranged them around the front door of their house. Henry set out the Nativity scene on a table in the living room. The crèche pieces were very old—they had belonged to Henry's father's mother when she was a little girl—and Henry handled them with great care and worried that Amelia Earhart would knock them off the table. (But she didn't.)

Before Henry knew it, Christmas Eve had arrived. Henry's plan had failed (or at any rate, he was far behind schedule, since by now he should have had a fully trained, friendly, bathed dog for more than two months), and Henry was fairly certain his parents weren't going to surprise him with a dog the next morning. There had not been one more word of discussion about anything dog-related, from responsibility to fenced-in yards. Still, Henry couldn't help but feel the surge of excitement that washed over him every year at Christmas. Claremont was dancing with wreaths and trees and lights and snowflakes and candy canes, his class had held an end-of-term party to which their parents had been invited, Henry's house smelled of gingerbread and pine and peppermint, packages were piling up under their tree, vacation yawned ahead, that evening the Christmas parade would take place on Nassau Street, and today Henry and his parents would pay their annual visit to Henry's father's aunt Susan.

"Henry?" his mother called up the stairs. "Are you almost ready? We should leave in half an hour."

"I'm ready!" Henry called back. And he was. He had not forgotten his promise to himself to prove that he could be adult and responsible for more than twenty-four hours. To this end, he had dreamed up, created, and wrapped his present for Aunt Susan entirely on his own. This had taken a good deal of time. He hadn't wanted to give just anything to his great-aunt. He loved her and looked forward to his visits with her and had decided that a box of stationery or a dishtowel or a coffee mug would not do. He had thought about his aunt, who was old (as old as Grandpa Jack and Grandma Lucy, his mother's parents, although she didn't act very old), and about her life and her house, and then he had remembered how much Aunt Susan loved her dog, Maxie. Maxie was a small black dog of uncertain background who looked more like a poodle than any other breed. Susan had adopted him after he had shown up at a neighbor's house wearing a too-small collar with no ID tags, and suffering from fleabites and eye infections. Henry remembered Susan's saying that when she first met Maxie she thought he was beautiful, bites and infections and all, and she had fallen in love with him.

It was this memory that had given Henry the idea for Aunt Susan's present. Nearly every night in December, after he finished his homework, he had worked on a pastel portrait of Maxie. Then he made a cardboard frame for the picture and wrapped the gift in silver and turquoise, colors his aunt liked quite a bit.

Henry trotted down the stairs, dressed in khaki pants and a blue blazer, his hair neatly combed, the gift in his hand. "I'm ready," he announced to his parents.

"You look so handsome!" exclaimed his mother.

"What's in the package?" asked his father.

"A secret," said Henry. "You'll find out when Aunt Susan opens it."

The drive to Susan's took nearly an hour, and Henry wished he had a dog to keep him company. But he said nothing.

When at last they turned into Susan's driveway, Henry saw his great-aunt standing in the doorway. She waved heartily, and Henry rolled his window down and called, "Merry Christmas, Aunt Susan!"

"Merry Christmas!" she replied.

The inside of Susan's house was warm and smelled much like Henry's—of spices and evergreens and magic. Maxie was wearing a red bow on his collar and when he caught sight of Henry he ran to him, hindquarters wiggling, and jumped up and down until Henry sat on the floor and hugged him.

"My goodness," said Susan, eyeing the bag of gifts Henry's mother was carrying. "I hope those aren't all for me."

"They're for you and Maxie," said Henry from the floor.

"You'll spoil us," said Susan, who looked as excited as Henry felt.

"I'll put them under the tree," said Henry. "It's more fun to open presents if they've come from under the tree."

Aunt Susan disappeared into the kitchen to attend to lunch preparations, and Henry lifted the gifts out of the shopping bag one by one and arranged them beneath the boughs of the Christmas tree. He couldn't help peeking at the packages Susan had already placed there, and he read some of the tags.

Merry Christmas to Charlie from your old Aunt Susan

For Henry—Stay warm! Love, Aunt Susan (Henry prepared himself for a hand-knitted item.)

Warm greetings to Rebecca from Aunt Susan (So Aunt Susan had knitted something for Henry's mother as well.

Henry closed his eyes and hoped the items didn't match. But if they did, he knew better than to say anything other than "Thank you.")

To Henry from Aunt Susan—Merry Christmas! (This tag was taped to a big box, and Henry felt a prickle of excitement.)

Aunt Susan returned to the living room carrying a tray with four mugs. The tray was decorated with poinsettias and so were the mugs. Henry sighed. This was one of the best things about Christmas: It was everywhere. He noted a snowman blanket on the back of his great-aunt's couch. Christmas cards were strung around the doorway. Miniature lighted trees lined the windowsill. Red ribbons and ropes of evergreens cascaded down the banister. Christmas was magical, Henry thought, and maybe—just maybe—anything could happen.

His thoughts were drifting to Buddy when Aunt Susan said, "Let's have a Christmas toast," and handed around mugs of hot chocolate.

Henry drank his while sitting on the floor with Maxie in his lap.

"Well!" said Aunt Susan, jumping to her feet. "I think we should open presents next, don't you? We'll eat lunch afterward. Henry, do you want to play Santa and hand out the presents?"

"I do," said Henry, "but I don't want to disturb Maxie."

He looked down at the little dog, who had fallen fast asleep and was snoring delicately.

Susan grinned. "Maxie loves you. All right. I'll be Santa."

"Aunt Susan?" said Henry. "Open that one first, okay?"

"This blue one?" She withdrew it from under the tree and read the card. "From you, Henry? Thank you." She peeled back the paper, gently opened the box inside, and lifted out the portrait. "Oh," she said, a catch in her voice. "It's Maxie, isn't it? It's wonderful! And you made it yourself. Thank you, Henry."

"You're welcome," said Henry.

"I'm going to keep it right here in the living room where I can see it all the time. What a thoughtful gift." Aunt Susan kissed Henry on the cheek, and Henry saw his parents exchange a pleased glance.

One at a time the other packages were opened: A sweater, a board game, a bowl for Maxie with his name on it, several books, a pair of earrings, an enormous box of artist's supplies (that was the big box for Henry from Aunt Susan), a nightgown, treats for Maxie, a lavender scarf (Aunt Susan's knitted gift for Henry's mother), and a navy hat (Aunt Susan's knitted gift for Henry, who breathed a sigh of relief).

Lunch came next, their traditional Christmas Eve lunch of turkey soup and warm biscuits, and then Aunt Susan said, "Can you stay a bit longer? Shall we sit by the fire again?"

So they sat before the glowing tree, surrounded by their gifts, Maxie once again snoozing in Henry's lap.

"Well," said Aunt Susan in her hearty voice, "Henry, what was on your Christmas list this year?"

Henry, who had started to feel as drowsy as Maxie looked, jerked to attention and risked a sideways glance at his parents. "Um," he said after a moment, "I mostly asked for a dog."

"He gave us his list from two years ago," spoke up Henry's father. "He asked for a dog when he was nine—"

"I suspect," Aunt Susan interrupted, "that he's asked for a dog since then, too."

"I really, really, really want a dog," Henry couldn't help saying.

"But?" prompted Aunt Susan.

"But Mom and Dad always say no." Henry decided not to go into any details. Not now. Not on Christmas Eve with even the dim hope of finding a dog beneath his tree the next morning.

Aunt Susan frowned. "That would be because of Sunny, I suppose."

"Who's Sunny?" asked Henry.

Susan sat forward in her chair and clasped her wrinkled hands. She looked intently at Henry's father, and her frown deepened. "Charlie, you haven't told Henry about Sunny?"

"Who's Sunny?" asked Henry again.

"She was your father's dog," replied Aunt Susan, and now she sounded puzzled. But there was something else in her tone, something Henry couldn't quite identify. He half expected Susan to shake a scolding finger at his father, and so he scooted backward in his chair, jostling Maxie. "She was one of the finest dogs ever," Susan continued. "But Charlie, *you* should tell Henry about her."

"It doesn't seem like much of a Christmas story," said Henry's father stiffly, and he glanced around the room, not looking directly at anyone until his gaze settled uncomfortably on Maxie.

Henry raised his chin and saw that his mother was slowly peeling apart a length of Christmas ribbon, as if this required great concentration.

"It isn't," said Susan, and her voice had softened. She offered a small smile to Henry's father. "But the boy wants a dog, and he deserves to know why you won't let him have one."

Henry was suddenly brimming with questions for his father. "Dad?" he said.

His father held up a hand. "Let me think for a minute."

Henry looked down at Maxie in his lap. Everything was very still, the only sound the strains of "Silent Night," which floated to Henry's ears from some other room in the house.

Finally, his father said, "This was back when I was just a little younger than you. When I was in fifth grade."

"Was RJ still alive?" asked Henry.

His father shook his head. "No. And that's an important part of the story." He gazed into the fireplace before turning around and facing Henry. "Although we lived on the farm we didn't have many animals," he began. "Just your grand-mother's chickens and Sunny. Sunny was RJ's dog. Well, she was our family dog, but she was devoted to RJ. She was about six years old when he died."

Henry nodded, stroking one of Maxie's silky ears.

"For a while, Sunny was very lonely without RJ, but gradually she began to follow me around, just the way she had followed my brother." Henry's father straightened in his chair and now he looked directly at Henry, as if they were the only two people in the room.

"She became your companion," spoke up Aunt Susan.

"Yes. She became my companion. She waited for me at the school bus stop and we took walks together and she slept in my bed. She was always by my side. She didn't take RJ's place for me and I didn't take RJ's place for her, but each of us helped the other to heal after his death. Sunny helped my parents too. By the time RJ had been gone for a year, we were beginning to feel like ourselves again—a changed family, but a restored one—and Sunny had played a role in that.

"Then, just before Thanksgiving the year I was in fifth grade, Sunny was running around on our property and a hunter shot her."

Henry opened his mouth in horror. "But—"

"And that was the end of Sunny," his father said quickly as if he couldn't wait to finish the story. "We buried her, and we never got another dog."

"But why would a hunter shoot a dog?" asked Henry. "Did he do it on purpose?"

"No, of course not. At least, I don't think so. He was hunting too close to our land and it was nearly dark. I suppose he saw Sunny moving and thought she was a deer and he took a shot. Which is exactly why people shouldn't go hunting. When the man realized what he had done, he ran off into the woods, never owned up to his mistake."

"His *mistake*?" exclaimed Henry. "It sounds more like a crime."

Charlie Elliot was sitting perfectly still, but his eyes were soft now, and he said, "The point is that losing Sunny was horrible."

"And you don't want Henry to go through what you went through," said Aunt Susan quietly. She had settled back in her chair, and her eyes, like Charlie's, had softened. "Isn't that right? It was painful and you want to spare Henry that pain."

Mr. Elliot didn't answer.

Henry looked at his mother who set aside the frayed ribbon, but said nothing.

"Do you have any pictures of Sunny?" asked Henry.

"Probably. Somewhere," his father replied.

"Maybe we can look for them sometime."

When there was no answer to this either, Henry understood that his father had said all he intended to say about Sunny, at least for the time being, and he fell silent. The conversations he had had with his parents about dogs made more sense now. Small indoor pets, such as Amelia Earhart and the hamsters, were safe. They didn't go outdoors so they couldn't run away or get hit by cars or shot by hunters. Dogs were another story.

Henry understood something else. There would be no surprise dog under the tree the next morning. He could let go of his last shred of hope. He was sad, but he understood.

The Christmas visit came to a quiet end. Henry and his parents packed up the gifts from Aunt Susan, climbed into their car, and drove silently home along snowy roads. Henry gazed out the window and thought about Buddy. Buddy who had stuck around Claremont, but who still foraged for garbage and slept... where? Henry didn't even know where Buddy slept. He hoped he found warm places.

The Elliots pulled into their garage, and Henry took his gifts upstairs to his room. He crawled under his bed and pulled out the Rehabilitation Plan, the leash, the collar, and a stash of dog biscuits. He considered the leash and collar for several moments before placing them in a box and wrapping it in star-covered paper.

Then he threw the Rehabilitation Plan in his wastebasket.

But he kept the cookies. He still intended to be Buddy's friend.

15. HENRY

With the ringing of bells on Nassau Street and a sharpening of the chilly air, Christmas Eve arrived. These hours before Christmas Day itself, Henry's favorite hours of the entire year, were so filled with anticipation and promise, that they seemed magical, even if Henry didn't actually believe in magic.

The bells sounded as darkness was gathering, and as soon as Henry and his parents heard the chimes, they put on their warmest clothes and walked to town. Nassau Street was already crowded with cheery people bundled into their coats and leggings and boots and mittens. Henry wore the hat Aunt Susan had knitted for him, and his mother wore her new scarf.

"Remember last year?" said Henry. "Remember when Santa drove the fire engine through town?"

Each year Claremont's Christmas parade heralded the arrival of Santa Claus, and each year Santa's arrival was memorable. Henry considered himself far too old to get excited about Santa Claus, but every time he thought about the parade he felt the same growing excitement he had felt when he was a very little boy, and he knew that Santa's surprise arrival was anticipated as eagerly by the adults in town as by the children.

Henry and his parents stood on the sidewalk in front of the library. They peered down Nassau until at last Henry said, "I hear music!"

The parade had begun. It was led off by a huge sleigh, outlined in winking lights and manned by elves who tossed candy into the crowd. Henry caught three chocolate bells and a peppermint drop. Several more floats rolled by and then Henry heard a chant of "Santa! Santa!" He joined in, the chant growing louder until someone behind Henry exclaimed, "There he is!"

"Where? Where?" said Henry.

A spotlight had been turned on and Henry saw that it illuminated the flat roof of the hardware store, where an enormous fireplace and chimney had appeared. As Henry watched, a pair of boots dropped down from inside the chimney, followed by a red-suited body. Santa landed on a pile of logs, crawled out of fireplace, and waved to the crowd. "Merry Christmas!" he called.

Henry, grinning, turned to his parents. "That's it, then," he said. "Christmas is officially here."

Henry and his parents walked home after the parade, Henry feeling as though he were somehow glowing. Snow was falling, his stomach was pleasantly full of chocolate, and he could still hear bells ringing. After supper, Henry's mother went to the attic and returned with the three stockings Aunt Susan had knitted the year Henry had been born. His father lit the fire, Henry read "The Night Before Christmas" aloud because it was a family tradition (he had a feeling he would still be reading it aloud when he was in high school), and then the stockings were hung and the evening was over.

"Bedtime," said his mother. "It's been a long day."

"Ten more minutes?" asked Henry. "Please?" And without knowing he was going to do so he walked through the kitchen, opened the back door, and looked out into his yard. Snow was piling softly around tree trunks and the garden shed. The raw air made Henry shiver, but he didn't move. After a moment his eyes drifted to the sky, but they returned to the earth when a dim shape emerged from the snow and began to steal across the yard.

Buddy.

Henry reached into his pocket and found a cookie. He always carried dog cookies these days. "Buddy?" he called softly.

Buddy halted, startled.

"It's okay. It's just me." Henry stepped into the yard in his slippers and bathrobe, and held out the cookie.

Buddy relaxed and scuffed through the snow to Henry, who patted him on his head. Then he took the cookie gently and ate it, his brown eyes trained on Henry's face.

164

"Would you like another one?" asked Henry, realizing he would have to go all the way upstairs to his room to get more, but Buddy was already disappearing into the snowy darkness.

"Good night," Henry called after him.

Henry awoke on Christmas morning to see dim gray light at the edges of his window shades. Either it was very early (in which case his parents would make him wait before dashing downstairs to see what was under the tree), or it was still snowing. Henry sat up, pulled the shade aside, and saw snow flinging itself against the window. Heavy snow. A Christmas blizzard. He couldn't even see Matthew's old house across the street. This was exciting—but where was Buddy? What did stray dogs do during blizzards?

Henry peered at his clock. Seven-thirty. This was the latest he had ever managed to sleep on Christmas morning. His parents were probably already awake. Henry opened his door and leaned into the hallway.

"Mom?" he called. "Dad? Merry Christmas! I'm up."

"Merry Christmas, sleepyhead," replied his mother. "Dad's downstairs. He's made a fire and started breakfast. We were just waiting for you."

Henry hugged his mother. He ran down the stairs and hugged his father. Stockings were to be opened first, but Henry—even after the conversation at Aunt Susan's—couldn't help glancing under the Christmas tree. How thrilling it would be to see, sitting excitedly among the wrapped gifts, a wriggling puppy. And next to the tree a wooden doghouse, just like the ones in cartoons, with a peaked roof and a cutout door and SPARKY or BUSTER or, well, BUDDY written above the door. But there was no dog and no doghouse and undoubtedly nothing else for a dog either.

Henry wasn't surprised. He wasn't even very disappointed. He had just wanted to check.

The morning passed pleasantly. Henry and his parents opened their stockings. Henry was amused to see that his parents had secretly hung a stocking for Amelia Earhart and filled it with new cat toys and a package of something called Feline Greenies (in Savory Salmon Flavor), which Amelia seemed to enjoy quite a bit.

After breakfast, the gifts under the tree were unwrapped. There were clothes for Henry and more drawing supplies, two new biographies of baseball players, and an elaborate hamster habitat for Carlos Beltran and Hamlet. A package with a tag reading "For Henry from Grandma Lucy and Grandpa Jack" revealed a complicated mechanical bank. When Henry handed pennies to a baseball player, its metal arm lobbed the coins into a dugout, where they disappeared into the base of the bank for safekeeping. Henry wished he could run across the street, as he used to do, to see Matthew's gifts, and then bring Matthew home so he could show him the bank and the habitat and the books. Instead he stood at the window and looked out at the snow. It was now piled high, but seemed to be falling more gently, and Henry was glad. He had an errand planned for the afternoon.

After lunch Henry's father sat in an armchair by the fire. He was wearing his pajamas and a new sweater, and poking through a box of chocolates. "I think this is the most relaxing day of the entire year," he remarked.

Henry wanted to ask him if they could look for photos of Sunny, but when he opened his mouth he found himself saying instead, "I think I'll go outside for a while."

"Good idea. It isn't every year we have a snowstorm on Christmas."

When Henry left his house, wearing all his warmest clothes including the hat from his great-aunt, he was carrying a plastic shopping bag, which he hoped his parents wouldn't ask him about. They didn't. "I'll be back later," Henry called.

He stood on his snow-covered porch and looked at the place where the steps should be. He couldn't see them at all, so he slipped and slid and finally jumped into a drift below, surprised to find that it came up over his knees. The plows had been down Tinker Lane, but no one had shoveled their walks or driveways yet, and the street was eerily quiet.

Henry wished for Buddy at his side. If Buddy were with him, Henry could talk to him as he slogged along to Letty Lewis's house. But he was on his own. He clutched the bag and when he reached the road in front of the lavender house he paused to study it. Most of the windows upstairs were dark, but the ones on the first floor were lit and glowed in the dim afternoon light. Henry wondered if Letty Lewis had guests. He'd never seen anyone at her house, but this was Christmas Day. She might have guests. What should Henry do then?

He was still standing in the road when the door of the house opened and Letty leaned out and called, "Henry Elliot? Is that you? Merry Christmas! What are you doing out there?"

Henry waved from the road and held the bag aloft. "Merry Christmas!" he called back. "I came to visit. I have something for you." He waded through the snow where he thought her driveway and front walk might be, at last arriving on the wide porch.

"What a lovely surprise," said Letty.

Henry cautiously climbed the slippery steps, stood by the door, and tugged his boots off. Then he edged inside. He hadn't been in Letty's house before. The first thing he noticed was that she didn't have guests after all. She seemed to be celebrating Christmas by herself. A tree, decorated with gold balls and giant red and green lights—Henry had never seen tree lights that size—stood in the corner, several presents arranged beneath it. But the house was still. Even the fire in the hearth had burned out.

"Um," said Henry after Letty had taken his wet coat and scarf and hat and hung them in a closet. "Well . . ." He held the bag toward her. "I wanted to give you this."

"My," said Letty, and for one brief horrible instant, Henry thought she was going to cry. Her voice had wobbled and her eyes filled with tears, but then she straightened up and said matter-of-factly, "I'd better open this by the Christmas tree," and Henry expelled an enormous sigh of relief. He and Matthew had long ago decided that there was almost nothing worse than a crying adult.

"Have a cookie," said Letty, pointing to a plate on a table beside an armchair.

"Thank you," said Henry, and he helped himself to a gingersnap, which he knew had come from the store. *Next year*, he said to himself, *I'll tell Mom we should make cookies for Letty.*

"Now," said Letty, settling herself before the fire, "let's see what this is."

She tore away Henry's wrapping to find Buddy's collar and leash. "Thank you!" she exclaimed, genuinely pleased. "But what—"

"I know you don't have a dog," said Henry quickly. "Yet. But the Rehabilitation Plan is sort of behind schedule, and then yesterday—" He stopped talking when he saw the confusion on Letty's face and he started over.

Henry told Letty about the Rehabilitation Plan, including the fact that he had retrieved the crumpled paper from his wastebasket. He told her that he hadn't had nearly as much luck with Buddy as he had hoped he would, but that it barely mattered because even if he succeeded, Henry now understood why his parents—in particular, his father—had really been saying no to a dog, and it had nothing to do with good behavior or expense or housebreaking or responsibility.

"And you don't want to try to talk to your father again? Now that you know about Sunny?" asked Letty Lewis.

Henry shook his head. "It will just make him sad. When I talk about getting a dog, he's thinking about Sunny and what happened to her and how much that hurt him."

Letty pursed her lips and nodded thoughtfully.

"So if I can't have a dog, I think you should have one," Henry continued. "You should have Buddy. I know I can train him. It's just taking longer than I thought it would. Maybe you could help me, if you want. And then when Buddy is all trained, I'll—I'll bring him to you."

Letty had unpursed her lips and was smiling now, but only with her mouth, not with her eyes. "Henry," she said, "this is the kindest gift I've ever been given and I do thank you for it. I can't tell you how touched I am that you thought of me, and of trying to help both Buddy and me. It's just that"—Letty paused—"I've never had a dog."

"But you have to take Buddy! You'll be surprised," said Henry. "A dog is great company." (Henry had almost added, "He'll keep you from being so lonely," but stopped himself in time.) "A dog will sit on the porch with you and follow you around the yard. You can talk to a dog and he'll look right into your eyes like he's listening to you." Henry thought of Amelia Earhart who was sweet, but didn't often seem to pay attention to what Henry said to her. She tended to let her gaze drift somewhere far, far away. "Plus, dogs will sleep in bed with you and curl up on the couch with you and even play games with you. A dog is an automatic friend. I promise."

"Henry," said Letty, "do you know, I think you are the most thoughtful boy I've ever met. I will cherish the collar and the leash, and more important, your reason for giving them to me. Let's work on Buddy—you and I—and see what happens, all right? Buddy certainly is a lucky dog to have someone like you looking out for him. And I'm a lucky old woman to have you for a friend. Let's just take things one step at a time and get Buddy trained first."

"Okay," agreed Henry. "Anyway, a secret outdoor dog is better than no dog at all."

When Henry left Letty Lewis's he looked up and down Tinker Lane and had just begun walking slowly in the direction of Nassau Street, dragging his toes as he did so, when he heard a shout. He turned and saw Antony and Sal trying out a new snow saucer in their front yard.

"Henry!" called Antony. "Hi, Henry!"

And Sal added, "Come see what we got."

Henry hurried to their yard, which, covered in snow, looked exactly the same as every other yard on Tinker Lane. He waved to the boys, and then to Sofia, who was standing on the front stoop wearing a tutu and snow boots, and proclaiming, "This has been the most wonderfulest Christmas ever in the history of the world. I got a whole ballet costume!"

Antony gave Henry two turns on the snow saucer, and then Sal said again, "Come see what we got." He tugged Henry inside, and Henry spent the next hour looking over the gazillion presents that Antony and Sofia and Sal and Peter and Ginny had received. When Henry returned to his own house later that afternoon he felt unusually content. It really had been a wonderful Christmas.

Henry had just one gift left to give now, and he retrieved it from his bureau drawer and tiptoed downstairs and through the kitchen without being seen by his parents. He opened the back door and looked into the yard. "Buddy?" he called softly. He stepped a few inches from the stoop. "Buddy?"

Buddy didn't appear. Henry scanned his yard and the

one next door and then tried to see into the woods that stretched up the mountain. Nothing. He looked down at the bag of fancy dog cookies tied with a striped ribbon. He sighed, then opened the bag and placed three of the cookies a little distance from the door.

"Merry Christmas, Buddy," he said.

The next morning, the cookies were gone.

16. HENRY

January arrived. Christmas was over and New Year's Eve had come and gone and school had started again. Ordinarily, Henry found this time of year somewhat dreary. He always seemed to catch the flu in January, and at school the playground became so slushy that often the teachers decided to hold recess in the gym or the cafeteria or worst of all, their classrooms. But this January, Henry had a project. He had Buddy.

Something amazing had happened after Christmas. Buddy had begun coming to Henry's yard at least once a day. Henry wanted to believe that maybe there was something to Christmas magic after all, or that maybe some sort of power had been released into the atmosphere when his father had finally told him about Sunny, and this power had called to Buddy. But he had a feeling that the truth was much more mundane: Buddy liked the new cookies Henry had bought for him. Before the cookies, Buddy came around whenever he felt like it. After the cookies, Buddy showed up at least once a day. In fact, he came by so often that Henry was afraid his parents might notice him. At the same time, he worried about what would happen when he ran out of the cookies. After all, he didn't want Buddy to *stop* coming around either, and he hadn't seen those particular cookies in the pet store until just before the holidays, so he had a feeling they were limited-edition treats. He had gone back to the store several days after Christmas and found one more bag of them, which he bought. But they wouldn't last forever.

"You guys," Henry said to Antony and Owen as they walked to school one morning, "I have to tell you something. It's about Buddy." Henry drew in a deep breath and told his new friends the whole story of Buddy, from the first time he had seen him by the garbage cans (which his friends already knew about anyway) straight through to the special cookies that were running out.

"Wow," said Antony.

"Yeah, wow," said Owen.

"So what do you think I should do?" asked Henry. "I only have half a bag of the cookies left. Buddy comes to my yard all the time now. I should be working with him every chance I get—before the cookies run out. I'll bet I could get him all trained for Letty Lewis in just a few weeks. The only problem is that I can't exactly work with Buddy in my yard."

"Yeah, your parents might see," said Antony.

Henry nodded.

"Um, Henry, why . . ." Owen paused and glanced sideways at Antony. "Why do you want to give Buddy to Letty Lewis?"

"Because she needs him," said Henry. "She's lonely and dogs are the best company."

"Uh-huh," said Owen.

"Well, anyway," said Antony, "no matter what you're going to do with Buddy, I guess that first of all you have to finish training him. Do you still have your—what did you call it?"

"The Rehabilitation Plan," said Henry. "I have it."

"Maybe you could train Buddy at my house," said Antony.

Henry brightened. "I could lead him over to your yard with the cookies," he said.

And he did. The first time Henry coaxed Buddy through the backyards to Antony's house, holding out one of the precious limited-edition cookies, Buddy followed him as though he'd been Henry's dog since he was a puppy.

Then Henry did a very daring thing. He made a shelter for Buddy under the eave of the back wall of the garden shed in his yard. He knew his parents might find it. But he thought there was a better chance that Buddy would be living with Letty Lewis by the time his parents had any reason to go to the shed in all this cold, snowy weather.

Using the cookies as rewards, Henry, now with the help of Owen and Antony, patiently taught Buddy to come when he was called and to sit. Buddy allowed them to hug him and even to hold him in their laps.

"I think," said Henry one Wednesday afternoon, "that we should get the collar and leash back from Letty Lewis. I think Buddy's ready to try them now."

Once again Henry caught a look between Antony and Owen. "What?" said Henry. "What?"

"Did you say *we* should get the collar and the leash back from Miss Lewis?" asked Owen. "Because I'm not going over to her house. She's too weird."

"I'm not going either," said Antony.

Henry considered asking them if they were scared, but thought better of it. "I'll go myself," he said.

"Good luck with that," said Antony.

Henry left the boys in Antony's yard, ran down the street, and knocked on Letty's door. When she opened it, he told her the good news about Buddy.

"And to think you did this all on your own," exclaimed Letty.

"Well, I had a little help," said Henry.

Letty handed him the collar and the leash, and once again Henry hid them under his bed, in safekeeping for the next day's lesson. That night he left a cookie outside the back door as usual, and tried to send a thought to Buddy, who he hoped was asleep in his shelter behind the shed. "Buddy," he whispered, "tomorrow is going to be a very big day for you. You have to try to be cooperative and patient and brave. If you can do that, and learn to walk on the leash, then pretty soon you'll have a real home."

But the next morning Henry was surprised to find the cookie exactly where he had left it. It was untouched. Henry snatched it before his parents could see it, then replaced it just before they all left for the day. When he returned from school, it was still there.

Uh-oh, thought Henry. *This is a problem.*

It was a big problem, he felt, but he didn't know what to do about it. He couldn't talk to his parents, so he ran to Antony's house.

"Have you seen Buddy?" he asked Ginny when she answered the door.

Ginny scratched her left heel with the toe of her right sneaker. "I don't think so."

"But you're not sure?" Henry felt his hopes rise.

Then Antony came to the door and said that no, he hadn't seen Buddy since the day before.

"He didn't come to my house last night," reported Henry. "Or if he did, he didn't eat the cookie. And he didn't eat it today either."

"Uh-oh," said Antony.

"I know," said Henry.

"Well, maybe he found some really good food somewhere and he doesn't want to leave it," suggested Antony. "I'll bet he's not far away. I'll bet he'll be back tomorrow."

"Probably," said Henry.

That night Henry left the same cookie out for Buddy, and the next morning it was still there. It was there after school too.

"Okay, this is serious," Henry told Antony and Owen. The boys were sitting on the stoop in front of Antony's house. The steps had been shoveled after the last snow, but they were still wet, and everything on Tinker Lane looked melty, slushy, and gray. "The last time I saw Buddy was Wednesday," Henry continued. "Today is Friday—and he hasn't stayed away overnight since Christmas. Something must be wrong."

"Maybe," said Owen. "Or maybe he just decided to move on."

"No. Not now. Not after all this time. Buddy was here to stay."

Henry felt like burying his head in his arms. He had absolutely no idea what to do, and he had a feeling this was a problem he couldn't solve on his own. If Matthew still lived here, Henry would have talked to him. They would have sat on Matthew's stoop in the cold and the wet and one of them would have come up with an idea. But Matthew was gone, his empty house an unpleasant reminder.

Henry didn't know Antony and Owen well enough to bury his head sadly in his arms, so instead he said, "Do you think maybe you guys could help me with Buddy?"

"Sure," said Owen.

And from behind them a voice said, "You should organize a search party." The boys turned to see Sofia standing in the doorway.

"Hey! That's a good idea," said Antony. "And we should leave cans of food around. Maybe he'll smell the food and come back."

"*If* he can," said Sofia darkly.

Henry ignored this. "It's a good thing he knows his name and that he learned to come when we call."

"I'll go find Sal and Peter and Ginny," said Antony.

"Maybe Mackey Brannigan can help us," added Owen.

"Maybe Letty Lewis can help too," said Henry.

Antony groaned. "Letty? Really? Isn't she kind of old?"

Henry shrugged. "Let's ask her anyway."

Half an hour later Henry was standing on Letty's porch. Behind him, stretching back to the street, were Owen, Antony, Mackey, Sofia, Salvatore, Ginny, and Peter. Everyone was carrying something: dog chow, cans of dog food, the limited-edition cookies, Buddy's leash, and his collar.

"My goodness. What's all this?" asked Letty when she answered the doorbell.

"Buddy's missing," Henry announced.

Letty put her hand to her cheek. "Oh, no. Are you sure?"

"The last time I saw him was Wednesday afternoon."

"And now it's Friday," said Letty thoughtfully.

"He's been coming to my house every single night," Henry told her. "To eat these." He held out the bag of cookies. "So I think something might be wrong."

"We've organized a search party," said Sofia, stepping forward hesitantly.

"And we're going to leave food all over the place for Buddy," spoke up Sal.

"Do you want to help us?" asked Henry.

"Well," said Letty. "I . . ."

Henry realized that Letty was wearing a bathrobe and a pair of moccasins. Her hair looked a bit wild.

"I want to help, but I'm not sure I'll be much good at searching," confessed Letty. "I could put some food around my yard, though. Just let me get dressed."

Henry left Letty with two cans of food and a supply of chow, and he and the others returned to Antony's house.

"This will be Command Center," said Owen. "Henry, you give out the orders."

"Oh," said Henry. "Okay. Um, let's see. There are eight of us. I think we should divide into three teams. Antony, you come with me. Owen, you'll be in charge of Peter and Ginny. Salvatore and Sofia will report to Mackey. Everybody, make sure you take some food with you. Mackey, your team will stay here in our neighborhood. Owen, you guys go into town. Antony and I will look in the yards around Caldwell Street." Henry checked his watch, feeling very official. "Meet back here in one hour exactly."

"Hey, what do we do if we find Buddy?" asked Mackey. "We only have one collar and leash."

"Good point," said Henry. He thought for a moment. "Well, two teams will just have to use rope. We have some in my garage. But be really careful with it, okay? Put it around Buddy's middle, not his neck, and don't tie it too tight."

Fifteen minutes later the teams set out. Henry and Antony, carrying a bag containing food, cookies, the leash, and the collar, walked through Antony's backyard and into the backyards of the houses on Caldwell Street. They peeked behind garbage cans. They peered into garages.

"Maybe someone went away on a trip and Buddy got locked in the garage," said Henry. But most of the garages they saw were open. And Antony pointed out that they couldn't check all the garages in Claremont anyway.

At the edges of several yards, Henry and Antony furtively left cans of food or small piles of dog chow.

"Don't let anyone see you," said Henry in a low voice. "And sort of hide the food. It might attract raccoons, and people won't like that."

They asked anyone they met if a medium-size tan dog

with short fur and brown eyes had been seen in the neighborhood. But the reply was always a shake of the head or a "No, sorry."

When they had been searching for forty-five minutes, Antony sighed and said, "I guess we should start back now."

"Let's leave a trail of chow behind us," suggested Henry, no longer caring about raccoons. "Buddy might find it and follow it back to my house."

"I guess," said Antony. He sounded doubtful, but they carefully sprinkled chow all the way back to Buddy's shelter in Henry's yard.

"There are the others," said Antony a few moments later, squinting down Tinker Lane. The search parties had returned.

"Anything?" Henry asked, running to his friends.

In answer, six heads swiveled slowly from side to side.

No.

An uncomfortable chilly sensation blossomed in Henry's stomach and spread down his arms and legs. He wasn't cold. In fact, all the activity had made him hot and sweaty. But he realized he was very afraid.

The chill that settled into Henry made him feel numb. He couldn't eat his dinner. And he found that he didn't want to do anything that evening except peer out into the murky nighttime, hoping to see Buddy lope through the backyard.

At eight o'clock he told his parents he was going to bed. They exchanged a look of concern.

"I think you're coming down with something," said his mother, resting her cool hand on his forehead. "You don't seem to have a fever, though."

"Anything the matter, son?" asked his father.

Henry shook his head, then fled to his room before tears could begin to fall. He turned out the light and knelt on his bed, now hoping to see Buddy in the front yard, in the glow of a streetlight. Or maybe he was across the street at Matthew's! Maybe Buddy had discovered a way in and out of the empty house and had made a home for himself there. Henry's heart leaped. But then he realized that if Buddy were just across the street, he could easily come by for his cookies. He rested his head on the windowsill and began to cry quietly. It had been a long time since he had cried and he'd forgotten how hot the rush of tears would be and how his chest would ache.

When the hand touched his shoulder he jumped.

"Sorry," said his father softly. "Didn't mean to startle you."

Henry wiped his eyes on the sleeve of his pajamas. "I didn't hear you come in."

"Do you want to tell me what's going on?"

"I can't." Henry slid under the covers, and his father turned the light on.

"I think you'll feel better if you talk about it."

"Not necessarily."

"Are you in trouble?"

Henry shook his head.

"Is someone else in trouble?"

Henry looked miserably at his father. "Sort of."

"A friend? Someone at school?"

"The person isn't a person, exactly. The person is more of a dog."

There. He had said it.

"A dog is in trouble?" repeated Mr. Elliot. He looked puzzled. "What dog?"

"Buddy," Henry whispered.

"Henry, I think you'd better start at the beginning and tell me the whole story."

"Okay," said Henry, and he sat up straighter and said boldly, "I have a secret outdoor dog." And then the rest of the story poured out.

Mr. Elliot listened patiently. Henry waited for his father to reprimand him or scold him or at the very least point out that Henry had disobeyed him. But his father rested his hand on Henry's shoulder and nodded and occasionally asked a question.

At last, Henry, his voice wobbling slightly, reached the

end of the tale, winding up by saying that none of the search parties had seen any sign of Buddy. He traced his finger along a wrinkle in the blanket, glanced up at his father, and then looked down at his covers again. And then he burst into tears.

Mr. Elliot drew his son close and said, "You did a good thing, Henry. Tomorrow morning, as soon as it's light, I'll help you search for Buddy."

17. HENRY

Henry was sleeping soundly when he felt someone sit on the edge of his bed. He opened his eyes, but saw only inky darkness. "Dad?" he said.

"We need to get an early start," his father replied softly.

Henry realized that the sun hadn't risen yet. He raised himself onto his elbows and yawned. "Okay."

"By the time we eat breakfast it will be light enough to set out."

Henry and his father sat at the table in the kitchen and ate eggs and oatmeal and toast. In the east the sky was brightening, turning heavy, dull clouds from black to a deep gray. There would be no sunshine that day.

"Wear your warmest clothes," Mr. Elliot said as he and Henry cleared the table. "It's going to be raw."

"Where do you think we should look?" asked Henry. "Yesterday we looked on Tinker Lane and Caldwell Street and also in town."

"I think we should start with the woods," said Mr. Elliot.

Henry dressed for the long cold day ahead and opened

the front door. Behind him, the rest of the household was waking. He saw his mother at the top of the stairs in her bathrobe, her hair rumpled from sleep. Amelia Earhart was sitting on the bottom step washing her face with her eyes closed.

Henry reached up to touch the hat Aunt Susan had made. The wool was vaguely scratchy. He wore the hat frequently anyway, and today he hoped it would bring good luck, since his great-aunt was the one who had told him about Sunny, and Henry had a feeling that that moment on Christmas Eve was somehow responsible for this early morning adventure with his father.

Henry looked across the street at Matthew's house with its dead windows and unshoveled walk, the snow piled high at the bottom of the driveway. Above the house towered clouds so thick Henry thought he might be able to scoop out handfuls of them.

"We'll see you later," said Henry's father to his mother.

"Be careful," she replied.

Mr. Elliot closed the door softly and looked at the clouds. "They're talking about more snow," he said. Henry and his father made their way across the yard to the street, turned left, walked past the DEAD END sign, and managed to locate the snow-covered trail that led up the mountain. "Keep your eyes and ears open," Mr. Elliot told Henry. "Don't watch the trail, watch everything around you. Look for movement among the trees and listen for sounds."

"What kinds of sounds?" asked Henry.

"The crunching of leaves. Barking, whining."

They walked along in silence, breaking it only to call for Buddy. Henry's father was wearing a backpack containing dog food. Henry was wearing a backpack containing the lunch they had prepared. They looked and listened, and sometimes Mr. Elliot stood still and cocked his head or stared at things in the distance. Every so often they opened a can of food and dumped its contents near the trail. Henry's father refused to leave the cans in the woods. "We'll take them home and recycle them. It's not fair to the woods to leave our trash behind."

By noon they were more than halfway up the mountain. Henry was getting used to hearing nothing but their own calls and footsteps, the wind in the fir trees, the cawing of crows, the sudden crack of breaking twigs as a startled deer leaped away through the underbrush. He was hot and sweating and very hungry.

"Should we stop and have lunch?" asked his father.

"Yes!" exclaimed Henry, and Mr. Elliot laughed.

They found a large rock, swept it free of the snow—a layer as thin as a piece of paper—that had managed to find its way through the branches of the pine trees, and spread their lunch on the blanket Henry had packed in case Buddy needed warming up when they found him.

"This reminds me of when I was a boy and Sunny and I would take hikes through the woods," said Mr. Elliot.

"You and Sunny used to go on hikes?" asked Henry.

"Lots of them. I'd pack lunch and a book to read and we'd spend the afternoon—or sometimes the entire day—in the woods."

Henry was incredulous. "You and Sunny spent a lot of time in the woods?" When Henry thought of his father as a boy he pictured him as a younger, smaller version of his adult self—a ten-year-old librarian. He had never once pictured his father tramping through a forest with a dog, knowing woodsy outdoor things.

"Yes," said Mr. Elliot. "Especially after RJ died. We were both lonely then. And Sunny was my . . ."

"Your best friend?"

His father lifted his head but said nothing.

Henry followed his gaze. He squinted at the sky. "No snow yet," he said.

"We'd better pack up and get going. We'll only have a few more hours of daylight. Time to head home."

They left the trail and went slipping and sliding down the side of the mountain. Henry kept falling and grew very annoyed, but Mr. Elliot said there was no point in going back the way they'd come. "We'd be covering the same territory."

"What about the food?" asked Henry as they neared the bottom. "We have to check to see if Buddy ate it." His annoyance had turned to panic. They couldn't go home yet. They were supposed to have found Buddy by now. Henry was wearing his lucky *hat*. And searching with his *father*.

"We'll check some of the food tomorrow when we set out again."

"Tomorrow?" wailed Henry. "I thought . . ."

Mr. Elliot put his hands on Henry's shoulders. "Take it easy. We'll start over again tomorrow."

And they did. The threatened snow did not fall and Sunday dawned with a brilliant pink sky beyond the mountains. Once again Henry and his father set off with their laden backpacks. They started out on the trail so that they could look for the food.

"I know we left some here!" called Henry. "And it's gone!" He paused. "But Dad, a raccoon or something could have eaten it." He leaned down. "There are little tracks in the snow. *Little* tracks. Not Buddy's."

Farther along the trail they found the remains of some more food. "Bigger tracks here!" cried Henry. And then he shouted, "Buddy! Buddy!" but there was no answering bark.

They left the trail then, traveling east instead of west, hiking along through snow and stumbling over rocks. By noon they were on a rise above town and they ate their lunch looking down at Claremont—at the streets and rooftops and treetops. "Hey," said Henry, "I can see our house from here." But he found no comfort in this, and when he turned to his father he felt his lip trembling. Only three or four more hours of searching were left and the next day was Monday. Back to school, back to work.

His father gave him a hug. Then he stood up. "Let's not waste the daylight."

Henry slogged along through the snow, trying to listen, trying to observe, trying to do everything his father was doing.

But the weekend was over.

"At least it didn't snow," said Henry.

"Buddy!" called Mr. Elliot.

"Buddy!" called Henry.

And from far away—on the other side of that boulder? Through those birch trees?—came a whine.

"Dad! Did you hear that?"

Mr. Elliot came to a stop and Henry stood beside him. They listened to the wind and listened and listened and Henry heard the whine again.

"Buddy!" he shouted. "Buddy!"

The whine grew louder and Mr. Elliot took off through the trees.

"Buddy! Buddy!"

The whine became a yip. A soft, sad yip.

"There he is!" cried Henry.

And there was Buddy. He had been lying in the snow and now he tried sit up—tried to sit just the way he had been taught—but he collapsed to the ground again.

"What's wrong with him?" asked Henry. He had thought that if they found Buddy he would run to him and throw his arms around him and feel his warm, strong body, but now he stood back. "Something's wrong with him, Dad."

"He's caught," said Mr. Elliot.

"What do you mean?" Henry took a step closer. "On what?"

"He's caught in a trap. A hunter's leg-hold trap."

Henry was afraid to look but still he crept forward until he was standing in front of his father.

"Don't touch him," said Mr. Elliot. "Not just yet. He's frightened. Let him smell you so he remembers you."

Henry bent over to peer at Buddy, who was trembling. The trembling turned to shaking, and he shook so violently that every part of his body seemed to vibrate.

"It's okay, Buddy," said Henry. "We're going to help you." He could hardly bear to look at the steel jaws that were clamped around Buddy's front paw, the metal biting through fur, through skin, making blood drip onto the snow where it froze into ruddy slush. Henry saw that all around Buddy the snow was stained with his blood. He had struggled mightily with his enemy, but now he lay still.

"Buddy," said Henry softly, "we're here. Remember

me?" He held out his hand, and Buddy sniffed it. He stopped shaking.

Henry turned around and looked up at his father. "How long do you think he's been here? If he's been in this trap since Wednesday—"

"I don't think he's been caught for that long," said Mr. Elliot, but he sounded angry and something dark slid across his face, which made Henry sit back on his heels, surprised. Mr. Elliot softened then. "I'm sorry," he said. "It's okay, Henry. Buddy's going to be okay."

Henry nodded. He slipped his arms out of his backpack, reached inside it, and withdrew the blanket.

And his father knelt in the snow, removed one glove, and extended his hand to Buddy. Buddy looked into Charlie Elliot's eyes. Then he licked the tips of his fingers.

18. CHARLIE

Charlie gets lost in the eyes, the brown eyes as deep dark as chestnuts. The snow melts and the woods drift away and now he's running through a stubbly autumn field holding fast to a spool of string as his kite jerks back and forth in the wind.

Charlie is proud, very proud, of this kite. He worked hard on it and he wanted RJ to be proud of it too—RJ who only smiled when Charlie told him he was going to make a kite all by himself. But Charlie made it anyway and he did a good job and here it is, sailing high on this blustery day. Charlie runs, lets the string out, changes direction in the field, runs some more, reels the kite back in. It is a kite masterpiece, but Charlie is the only one who knows this.

He lets the string unwind again and now the kite looks impossibly tiny. Charlie sees that he has let out too much string, the whole spool, and far ahead of him the kite begins a plunge toward the earth. Charlie stops. He can't reverse the kite's path this time, so he watches until his masterpiece is out of his sight and he's sure it has landed somewhere.

Then he bends over, hands on knees, and breathes in and out, in and out, until he stops panting.

When he has caught his breath, he follows the string in its looping path through the field, winding it around and around the spool, the spool growing fatter as Charlie nears the kite. He's approaching the barn when he hears branches breaking—a crash almost as loud as if an entire tree were toppling to the ground—and a cry and then that thump that he'll never forget. He pauses for just a moment, listening, and Sunny begins to bark and Charlie realizes that this is her bark that means something is wrong.

Charlie speeds up until he's running again, racing to the fir trees. He tosses the spool aside and forgets about following the string, instead sprinting in a straight line toward the trees, which is how he almost steps on the kite. It has landed near the barn door and has a large hole in it. Charlie lets out a cry at the sight of his ruined work of art. He snatches it up and that's when he sees the pile of clothes several yards ahead under the tallest of the trees, and then recognizes the clothes as RJ. RJ in a heap on the ground with Sunny standing over him.

"RJ!" Charlie cries.

Charlie has been moving so fast that he has a cramp in his side, and he's doubled over, running bent in two like a broken branch. He reaches his brother and drops the kite.

Charlie kneels down and suddenly everything is still.

Before, there were birdcalls and the relentless wind in his ears and the crash and the thump. Now he hears not a sound. He stares at RJ, who's as still as the rest of the stillness. Charlie sees a drop of bright red blood appear in the corner of RJ's mouth and then it's a trickle, running down his cheek. Another drop appears in his nose and begins a second trickle that joins the first, finally spilling onto the ground.

Charlie can't think. He sits back on his heels. Nothing at all is moving. Not the trees, not Charlie, not Sunny, and certainly not RJ. Charlie looks deep into Sunny's brown eyes. She holds his gaze and then at last she moves forward and licks Charlie's hand.

Charlie is galvanized into action. He leaps to his feet. "Stay!" he commands Sunny unnecessarily, since he can see that she's already guarding RJ. Charlie's side doesn't hurt quite so much now, and as he runs to the house he knows he's running faster than he has ever run in his life. He crashes through the front door, shouting, "Mom! Mom! Help!"

Mrs. Elliot is in the kitchen. She's just starting to prepare dinner. Her hands are poised above a bowl in which Charlie knows is ground beef mixed with an egg for a meat loaf. In a second bowl are beans, neatly sliced and ready to go into a pot as soon as Mr. Elliot returns from work that night. Mrs. Elliot is wearing an apron she made herself, an apron with a little pocket in the shape of a cat. The adult Charlie sees all this—sees the entire kitchen with the blue-and-white-checked curtains and the scarred wooden table and the red linoleum floor and his mother looking up in alarm—as clearly now, thirty-two years later, as he saw it when he was nine.

"What? What is it?" asks Mrs. Elliot. She's already wiping her hands on her apron and reaching for the phone.

"RJ fell out of a tree! He's not moving. You have to call the ambulance!"

Mrs. Elliot dials 0 and asks the operator for an ambulance and says it's an emergency and to hurry, hurry, please. She's remarkably calm, but the moment she hangs up the phone she runs out of the house, and Charlie is the one who notices that a burner is on and turns it off before he flies out the door after his mother. He follows Mrs. Elliot back to the fir trees, hoping that things might be different now. Maybe RJ will be sitting up, dabbing at the blood under his nose and laughing a little at the scare he gave everyone. Maybe Sunny will be bouncing from side to side in relief, her tail held high.

But the scene is barely different. RJ is lying in exactly the same position under the tree, the kite nearby. Sunny has lain down next to RJ and rested her head on his chest as she sometimes does on winter nights when she crawls into bed with him. She's begun to whimper.

Mrs. Elliot screams.

She falls to her knees and pats RJ's cheeks. She takes his wrist in her hands and tries to find his pulse.

"What happened?" she asks Charlie.

Charlie can already hear a siren in the distance. The ambulance is probably just leaving town. "I don't know," he says. "I heard a crash and I heard RJ shout and when I got here he was lying on the ground."

"Was he climbing after the kite?"

Charlie can't think. His brother is laid out before him, and Sunny won't get up and his mother is sobbing and the siren sounds closer.

"Go call your father," says Mrs. Elliot sharply. "He's working at the Landaus' today. Tell him to meet us at the hospital."

Charlie does this, but he's back outside by the time the ambulance arrives, so he hears the attendant say that RJ is already gone.

Lost. They've lost him.

The adult Charlie returns to the woods and the snow and his son and Buddy's soft tongue on his fingers. But RJ and Sunny and his mother and the fir trees are before him too, and so is the kite. Why had he not remembered that he carried the kite to RJ's side? But he remembers now and knows that RJ didn't climb the tree to rescue Charlie's kite. He climbed it because it was a nice autumn day and he didn't have a lot of homework and maybe he wanted to prove something to his friends or maybe he just wanted to see if he could do it.

The accident was not Charlie's fault.

"Dad?" says Henry now. "What do we do? How do we get the trap off of Buddy's leg?"

Mr. Elliot, heart beating noisily in his chest, sends the past soaring away like his kite. He sits for a moment, catching his breath, and he strokes Buddy's sleek head. "We should let a vet do that. We'll have to bring Buddy and the trap together to Dr. Burton's."

"Leave the trap on his leg?" cries Henry in dismay. "But he's bleeding!"

"It's the safest thing. Trust me. Now let's see where this chain goes." Henry's father indicates a chain trailing away from the trap. It leads to a stake in the ground. He pulls and tugs at the stake and finally manages to wrench it from the frozen earth. "You'll have to help me lift Buddy," he says to Henry. "I'll pick him up and you hold on to the trap."

They make their way slowly back to Tinker Lane. Mr. Elliot cradles Buddy, wrapped in the blanket, and Henry holds tightly to the trap, not caring that blood from Buddy's foot seeps through his mittens and onto his hands.

Once they reach their house, things happen more

quickly. Mrs. Elliot sees them coming and greets them at the front door. "Oh, no. Oh, poor pup," she says.

"We need to call Dr. Burton," Charlie tells her. "I hope he can go into his office on a Sunday."

Charlie bustles Buddy into the kitchen, Henry still gripping the trap. Henry's mother grabs two cushions from the couch and covers them with an old cloth, the one they use for painting projects, and Charlie and Henry lay Buddy there, trap and all. Then Charlie phones the vet.

"He'll meet us at the office," he reports when he hangs up. "We should leave right now."

So Buddy is bustled right out the door again and into the back of the Elliots' car where he rides between Henry and Mrs. Elliot, who pat him and talk to him. Henry never lets go of the trap. Charlie drives the car, and in no time they have pulled into Dr. Burton's parking lot.

"There's his car," says Charlie. "He's here already."

Inside, Buddy is lowered onto an examining table and finally Henry can remove his hands from the trap.

"Now," says Dr. Burton. "Let's see what we have here."

That night, after the trap has been removed from Buddy's leg and his wounds have been tended to and he's been settled into a crate at Dr. Burton's office, Charlie sits by the fire with his wife and his son. He and Henry have changed out of their bloody clothes, and they've all eaten a rather large dinner and are feeling sleepy.

"Dr. Burton said Buddy is a nice dog," remarks Henry. "He said he's well-behaved."

"Good-natured," adds Mrs. Elliot.

"He didn't make a sound when Dr. Burton removed the trap," says Charlie thoughtfully. "I think he must have lived with a family at some point. Otherwise he would never have let us pick him up. He was awfully good in the car too."

"I suppose we should try to find his owners," says Mrs. Elliot. "They must be missing him."

Charlie looks at his son. "Henry, how long did you say you've been feeding Buddy?"

"Feeding him and *training* him," Henry replies. "A long time. Since October, maybe. And Dad, I don't think anyone is missing Buddy. I haven't seen any lost-dog posters around."

"All the same, we should look for his owners," says Mrs. Elliot.

Charlie is watching his son. Henry has opened his mouth and wants to say something. Charlie knows he wants to ask if they can keep Buddy.

But Henry doesn't ask and Charlie doesn't offer.

19. **BONE**

I have been in pain many times during my life. I have stepped on sharp stones and I've stayed out in the snow too long. I hurt my nose when the man called George threw my sister and me out the window of the car. Once I was sitting on the floor next to Julie, the baby, and she grabbed my ear and pulled it so hard that I felt a sharp stab that seemed to shoot all the way through my head.

But the pain I felt when the trap closed around my foot, and even after Dr. Burton had removed the trap, was like no pain I had felt before. Dr. Burton gave me medicine to make the pain go away. I know this because he stuck me with a needle and said, "This is to help you feel better." And soon the pain disappeared. But then it came back. My foot throbbed and my body ached, and then I grew warm all over and Dr. Burton said to another doctor, "He seems to have developed an infection." So they gave me even more medicine.

When I was at Dr. Burton's I had to live in a cage in a room with lots of other cages in it. Each cage held a dog.

Some of the dogs were quiet and still. Some barked. The poodle in the cage next to me was very young and very bouncy and wanted to play, but I didn't feel like playing. And I didn't like my cage, although the people who came into the room with food and medicine were nice. They patted me and talked softly to me and the food they gave me was good. It smelled meaty and was spooned out of a can—a little can, not a garbage can.

The day after the boy and the man found me in the woods and brought me to Dr. Burton's, they came to visit me. It was the end of the afternoon and through a window above a table I could see that the sky was growing dark. A young woman with hair as long as Isabel's had just put food in all the cages so my belly was nicely full. I was feeling better. My body wasn't so warm and my paw wasn't throbbing as badly as it had been in the morning. I was resting on my side, my bandaged foot stretched out in front of me, when the woman with the long hair returned and as she walked toward my cage, she said, "Buddy, you have visitors."

Then I saw the boy called Henry. He was following the woman closely and as soon as he caught sight of me, he cried, "There he is, Dad!" He turned to the woman. "Can we touch him?" he asked.

The woman opened my cage and slowly Henry reached out his hand. "Hi, Buddy," he said softly. "How are you?" He patted my side carefully.

I stiffened at first and Henry drew his hand back quickly, but then I inched toward the front of the cage and Henry smiled and stroked me again. He let his hand run up and down my side and I thought maybe this is the way Estelle the cat would feel when she began to purr.

The man was standing behind Henry, looking in at me. "You gave us a scare," he said.

"How long until he's all well?" asked Henry.

"Hard to say exactly," replied the woman. "He developed a fever overnight, but he seems to be doing better now."

"Will he be able to walk again?"

"You'll have to ask Dr. Burton, but I don't see why not. After his wounds heal I think he'll be almost as good as new."

Henry patted me for a while and talked to me. "Did you know we sent out search parties?" he asked. "Owen and Mackey and Antony and Antony's brothers and sisters and I went looking for you. So did Letty Lewis, sort of."

Henry and the man who was his father left after a while, and then Dr. Burton came in. He looked into each cage. When he reached mine he said, "Well, well. You've had some excitement, haven't you, boy? You were lucky to be rescued."

The woman with the long hair appeared beside him and she said, "What's going to happen to him now?"

"I'm not sure yet," said Dr. Burton.

"Are the Elliots going to adopt him?"

"They haven't said so."

"If they don't adopt him, I'd like to take him home. He's an awfully sweet dog. Especially after all he's been through."

Dr. Burton smiled. "I wouldn't mind adopting him myself."

I looked out the window and all I could see now was nighttime. Dr. Burton and the woman left. The room with the cages grew dark and quiet.

I fell asleep.

When I awoke it was the next morning. I was hungry and not at all hot and my foot wasn't throbbing.

I had more visitors that afternoon. This time Henry came with his mother and with Antony and Owen.

"Buddy!" exclaimed Antony. "What happened to you? Your fur is all different."

"He had a bath," said Henry importantly. "Look how shiny he is."

The next few days were very much like this one. Henry visited every afternoon. I ate as much food as I wanted, and my foot stopped hurting unless I stood on it, and Dr. Burton said the infection was completely gone. One day when Henry was visiting he exclaimed, "Hey, I can't see your ribs anymore, Buddy. That's a good sign." Another day he said, "Tomorrow they're going to take off your bandage."

And that's exactly what happened. Dr. Burton had been changing my bandage all along, but each time he took it off and cleaned my wounds, he put a fresh one back on. Not this time, though. This time he removed the bandage and threw it away and then he held my paw in his hands and said, "You have a strong constitution, Buddy. You healed quickly. Now we just need to get you walking again."

He said something else too. He said, "You won't need to be here much longer. Soon you can go home."

I practiced walking with Dr. Burton. I walked back and forth in the big room with the cages. Then the woman with the long hair took me for walks outside. "You're doing well, Buddy," she said, and she patted me and kissed the top of my head.

One day Dr. Burton let me sit behind the reception desk in the front of his office. He told me I could be his greeter because I was friendly, and he let everyone who came into the office know that I was available for adoption. At the end of the day I slept in my cage again.

The day after that I was busy with my greeting duties when the door opened and in walked Henry and his father and his mother. Henry was holding a collar in one hand and a red leash in the other. And he was wearing a very big smile on his face.

Henry's father talked to the man at the reception desk and then to the woman with the long hair and finally to Dr. Burton, who joined Henry and his parents and me in the waiting room. Now Dr. Burton was smiling too, almost as widely as Henry, and he turned to me and said, "You are one lucky dog, Buddy. You have a home."

Henry was sitting next to me on the floor and he took my head in his hands and whispered, "You're going to come home with us."

When we walked out of Dr. Burton's office I was wearing the collar Henry had brought. The red leash was fastened to the collar, and Henry was at the other end of the leash. He helped me into the backseat of a car and as the car rolled along I sat up very straight and tall. Once when Henry looked at me he said, "Hey! Buddy's smiling!"

I gazed out the window, remembering rides in Franklin's car. I saw snow on the ground. I saw birds. I saw boys and girls playing on a street that looked familiar. I recognized garbage cans I had tipped over and eaten from.

The car slowed down. It turned a corner. And Henry's father said, "Here we are. Welcome to your new home, Buddy."

EPILOGUE

I sat in the yard and squinted into the setting sun. The air was hot. Even as the sun dipped below the horizon, the air was hot.

"Buddy! Come here, Buddy!"

Henry ran by me, chased by Antony and Owen. They were barefoot, wearing shorts and T-shirts. Sweat ran down their faces and necks. I leaped to my feet and tore after them. Henry laughed and I ran faster. I ran until I was ahead of him. Then I turned, skidding, and ran in the other direction, nearly crashing into Antony.

"Buddy is faster than a cheetah," exclaimed Owen.

I turned a second time, zipping back across the yard, and as I flew by Henry, he tapped my back and shouted, "Tag! You're it!"

I stopped short, and Henry and Antony and Owen fell to the ground in a heap. Henry wrapped his arms around me.

The back door opened then and Henry's father called, "Fifteen more minutes."

Henry flopped back in the grass and announced, "To-day is the longest day of the whole year."

I rested my head on his chest. Owen stroked my snout. Antony patted my ears.

"Summer vacation," said Owen.

"Swimming," said Antony.

"New neighbors tomorrow," said Henry.

We lay in the grass while the sky grew dark and the fireflies began to wink among the trees and the crickets chirruped and the bats came out.

From a distant yard a voice called, "Owen!"

"I have to go," said Owen.

"Me too," said Antony. "See you tomorrow, Henry."

I followed Henry into the house and up to his room. On the stairs I passed Amelia Earhart and I touched my nose to hers. She lowered her head, inviting me to lick it, which I did. Later, when Henry was reading in bed, his mother came into his room and set a fan on the desk. "You'll need this tonight," she said. She kissed Henry and kissed me and kissed Amelia, who was now asleep on Henry's feet.

Henry's father peeked into the room. "Good night, Henry," he said. "Good night, Amelia. Good night, Buddy."

"Night," said Henry.

I looked at Henry. He looked at me. Then he lifted the sheet so I could crawl underneath it. I lay pressed against

Henry while the fan whirred and Amelia purred and Henry read his book.

I dreamed of Henry and home.